I0607523

Perspective
Life's Outtakes - Year 15

52 Humorous and Inspirational Short Stories

By
Daris Howard

A collection of stories, humorous anecdotes, thoughts, and tidbits of wisdom from the newspaper column *Life's Outtakes*.

Publishing Inspiration

Perspective

Life's Outtakes - Year 15

52 Humorous and Inspirational Short Stories

By

Daris W. Howard

A collection of stories, humorous anecdotes, thoughts, and tidbits of wisdom from the newspaper column *Life's Outtakes*.

Copyright © 2021
by
Daris W. Howard

All rights reserved. No part of this book may be reproduced or transmitted in any form or by any means, electronic or mechanical, including photocopying, recording, or by any information storage and retrieval system without the written consent of the publisher.

ISBN-10: 1629860263
ISBN-13: 978-1629860268

www.publishinginspiration.com

Publishing Date: September 5, 2022

Publishing Inspiration LLC

Table of Contents

Dear Reader,

People often ask me if my stories are true. Though I admit that I tend to take a bit of literary license in my writing, each story is based on an actual event. Sometimes the stranger stories are the ones that are stretched the least. As people often say, truth is stranger than fiction.

I also want to note that some of the names have been changed to protect the anonymity of the individuals.

Daris Howard

A Cow Explained

A friend of ours came to visit. She had two little girls. Susan was five, and Tiffany was three. I enjoyed these two children. They were both cute and smart. But the things I enjoyed the most were that Susan talked like an adult, and she was a voracious reader. Though she was only five, she had probably read every children's book we had at our house during her visits. Why that was fun was because she didn't always understand everything she read, and her interpretation sometimes made more sense than the way we adults think and talk.

While their mother visited with my wife, Donna, the two little girls came out to swing on our swing set. I was working on a shed roof nearby, so Donna asked me if I could keep an eye on them. That was easy from my vantage point, so I agreed.

Susan was kind to her little sister, pushing her endlessly on a swing. But then they heard something and stopped to find out what it was.

Our cow, Leah, had seen the two girls. Always one to want to make friends and desiring to get her ears scratched, Leah had come to the fence and was calling to the girls.

Susan led Tiffany by the hand over to the fence. Leah put her head over, begging for attention.

"This is a girl cow," Susan said with a great air of authority.

"How d'you know?" Tiffany asked in her cute child voice.

Susan turned to me to verify that she was right. "Mr. Howard, this is a girl cow, isn't it?"

I nodded. "Yes, Susan."

Susan then turned back to her little sister. "I knew it was a girl cow because she has big eyelashes."

I had to smile at that. Naming the cow Leah was my wife's idea. Leah had big brown eyes and big eyelashes, and the Bible talks about Leah, the wife of Jacob, as having tender eyes.

Leah could not get the girls to scratch her ears, so she mooed at them. It was loud for the two little girls standing next to her. The sound scared Tiffany, and she backed away.

"You don't have to be scared," Susan said. "Cows have horns, and the sound they make comes from them opening their mouths and blowing their horns."

Susan led Tiffany back up to Leah and pointed at Leah's back end. "Do you see that big ball thing hanging on the cow's belly? That is called an 'under' because it hangs under the cow. And do you see those four pointing things hanging down from the under?"

Tiffany looked closely and nodded.

"Those are called treats," Susan said. "And do you know why they are called treats?"

Tiffany shook her head, hanging on to everything her big sister said.

"They are called treats," Susan continued, "because cows make cow pies, and then they give milk to go with pies. So, the cow pies and milk are treats."

Susan looked up at me. "Do you like cow pies, Mr. Howard?"

"I can't say as I have ever tasted one, so I wouldn't know," I replied. "However, I will admit that I once stuffed my cousin's face in one when he tricked me into touching an electric fence. He didn't seem to enjoy the cow pie, so I've never had a hankering to try one."

"Do you think Tiffany and I could taste one?" Susan asked.

"I'm afraid we're all out of warm cow pies right now," I replied. "But we do have some fresh milk that came from this cow's treats just this morning. Donna also made some chocolate chip cookies today. What do you say we go into the house and have some milk and cookies?"

The girls nodded, so I came down the ladder. The three of us scratched Leah's ears, then headed in for the cookies and milk. And indeed, it was a treat. But I knew I would never think of that word the same way again.

Proving Someone Right or Wrong

Mateo looked at the paper in his hand and smiled. He felt one of the greatest feelings of satisfaction he had ever felt. But then a memory came back to him—one that was a mix of both good and bad.

Mateo was only ten when he came to the United States. Most of his family had been there for quite a while. But when they immigrated, there hadn't been room for all of them. One person would have to stay behind.

Mateo's older brothers could get jobs and earn money to help the family once they moved. The ones younger than Mateo needed to stay with their parents. So, it was decided that eight-year-old Mateo would be the one who stayed behind. He would live with his grandparents until his father came to get him.

"I will be back soon, my son," his father said.

Mateo didn't mind staying behind. His grandparents were old, and it was hard for them to keep track of him. Sometimes he would be gone into the jungle for days. He wore very little and would live on the fruit he picked. He slept in the trees at night. It was a wonderful life.

Each time he returned to his grandparents' home, they scolded him. "Mateo, you should be living with us and going to school like other children." But nothing they said could change him.

A couple of years went by, and then one day, while Mateo was playing in the trees, he heard someone call his name. He looked down, and there stood his father.

"Mateo," he said, "I'm here to take you to the United States."

Mateo didn't want to go, but he knew better than to argue with his father. Mateo soon found himself in a strange country. His family members were all busy with their lives and had little time for him. Their language had changed, and he didn't always understand them. He also knew they didn't understand him. Sometimes his parents just nodded their heads as Mateo spoke, and he wondered if they even still spoke the same language.

He tried to stay out once on his own. But the food didn't just hang from trees everywhere he looked. There were flashing lights, sirens, and many strange things. And to top it off, his father came to find him and was not happy about Mateo not coming home.

School was even worse. The children would get him to do things they knew were wrong, though Mateo didn't. When he climbed a tree he was not supposed to climb, his teacher, Mrs. Doddson, was mad.

"Mateo," she said. "You will never amount to anything." And because she treated him that way, he believed it. Soon he was running with the wrong kids and getting into trouble. He even spent a few nights in jail. His father came to get him out of jail more than once.

Then one day, when Mateo was heading with his friends to steal from a store, his teacher, Mrs. Johnson, grabbed him. "Mateo," she said, "why do you do bad things with those kids? You know better. I can see better in you."

Mateo pulled away. "I like to be in control of my own life," he said.

"But are you, or are they in control of you?" Mrs. Johnson said. "You are only in control of yourself when you are reaching the best you can be. And you are not doing that with them. You can do better."

In some ways, Mrs. Johnson's words stung more than Mrs. Doddson's did because Mateo knew she was right. He thought a lot about what Mrs. Johnson said, and he started to change. He found new friends, Mrs. Johnson helped him learn to read, and soon he was doing well in school.

Mateo went on, working hard, and now, the paper he held in his hand was a college diploma. As he looked at the paper, he decided he needed to send a copy to each of his two teachers. He would send it to Mrs. Doddson to show her she was wrong. But he would send it to Mrs. Johnson to show her she was right. He was going to be a teacher and help others find the best in themselves, just as she had helped him.

The Undesirable Assignment

My friend, Ed, and I were visiting. Like me, he was a teacher at the university. I had just given an exam in my math class, and it had been open for five days. I had sent the students an email reminder each day, and I mentioned it in class all week. But as soon as it closed, five students emailed and said they didn't know they had a test to take. I was complaining about it to Ed, and he told me a story,

In his early years, while he was going to school, and for a while after becoming a professor, he had worked in the park service during the summers. He had often worked on trails. He would cut up fallen trees, build bridges, move rocks, and do other assigned tasks.

Ed usually worked alone on the trails and had become well known for his efficiency and how much he accomplished. That was why Ed was surprised when his supervisor called him into his office and told him he would have an assistant one summer. Ed expressed his disinterest in having anybody work with him.

"Oh, your assistant is not just anybody," Ed's supervisor said. "His name is David, and he's the son of the park superintendent. He's seventeen, and he has been rebellious toward his parents. His father has decided some hard summer work will be good for his son. The superintendent looked at the work record of our employees, and since you seem to get more work done than anyone, he said David is to be assigned to you."

Ed protested. "I'm only twenty-one, far too young to train someone."

"Look, Ed, I don't like this any more than you do. But I have no choice, and neither do you. However, the superintendent said for you not to worry if his son complains to him about you. He will not count anything negative David says against any of us. He also said he doesn't want you to go easy on David. He wants you to make him work hard and treat him like you would any other young man. Make him toe the line."

Ed reluctantly agreed to the assignment, and the next day he met David. David had all the swagger of a rebellious teen. David ignored most of what Ed said. Ed considered what to do, then went in and requested an assignment deep in the woods. When he explained his reasoning, the supervisor smiled and granted his request.

The next day, Ed showed David what to pack for their trip. They would have a four-day hike into the woods, several days for their work, then have a four-day hike out. They needed to have enough food, a tent, and sleeping gear. Ed packed his own pack while casually watching David ignore the advice he was given. Ed gave David a saw and an ax to add to his pack. When David declared he was ready, Ed winced, having seen what David had and hadn't put in. But no amount of talking made any difference, so they started on their journey.

They hiked all day, and when night came, they set up camp. They set up their tents, and then they sat down to eat. David had mostly packed junk food and ate candy bars and chips. Ed heated a military-style MRE.

"What's that junk?" David asked.

"It's called an M-R-E," Ed said. "It stands for meal ready to eat. Some people call it three lies in one."

"Well, it smells terrible," David said.

"It doesn't taste that great, either," Ed said. "But it's packed with nutrition, it's filling, and it isn't too heavy to carry."

"You won't get me to eat one of those," David said.

By the time they reached their destination, David was out of food. As Ed sat down to his meal, David asked if he had extra food.

"All I got are MREs," Ed said.

David turned away in disgust, but by the next morning, he was willing to eat anything. When he begged for some food, Ed nodded.

"But I will have to split my meal with you because we've got to have enough to get the work done and hike four days back out."

Ed was still hungry when he finished his half of the meal, and he knew he would be hungry for the whole assignment. But he also knew they would both survive, and his young assistant had learned his first lesson.

The Undesirable Assignment

(Part 2)

Ed worked for a national park in the summers. One summer, he was assigned to work with the park superintendent's son, David. Ed was only twenty-one, and David was a rebellious seventeen. David had refused to pack the food Ed told him to take, taking only snacks instead. So, by the time they reached their assigned work area after four days of hiking, David was already out of food. Ed ended up needing to share his food, which meant they were both hungry.

Besides the bucksaw and ax they each carried, Ed had a small chainsaw. On the fifth day out in the woods, they started to clean the trail. That is, Ed cleaned. David just moped and complained about the work and being hungry.

"Well, you know," Ed said, "if you would get in and work, we could get this job done sooner and get back to park headquarters."

"How long will it take us?" David asked.

"Probably three days if we work long hours, and if we both work," Ed said. "Five days if I have to do it alone. Then we'll have the four-day hike back."

David gasped. "I'm supposed to go hungry for seven days and do this stupid work, too?"

"Well, I'm going hungry, too, because you didn't pack what I told you to pack," Ed said.

David angrily jumped up. "I've had enough of this garbage. I'm heading back."

"And just how do you plan to do that?" Ed asked. "You have a four-day hike with no food, and you don't know the woods. You might get lost and not make it back."

"You should give me some food, and I will leave my pack so I can hike faster," David replied. "And I will just follow the trail."

Ed mulled that over a minute. If he gave David some food, would he just be enabling him? But if he didn't give him food, he could be blamed for David starving.

"All right," Ed said. "Since you will be hiking faster, I will give you what I would share with you for two days. That's all I can spare and be able to finish the job and hike out myself."

Ed gave David the food, and David complained it wasn't very much.

"I don't have very much because you didn't bring what you were supposed to," Ed replied.

Grumbling, David dumped everything else out of his pack. He then put back in the water and the food. He didn't even plan to carry his bedroll.

As David headed out, Ed yelled after him, "Don't forget your bear training in case you meet one."

Ed went back to work. He was hungry and wanted to get this job done so he could head back as well. He had just started cutting some small saplings with the bucksaw when he heard a scream. He turned to see David running across the meadow with a bear on his tail. David scurried up a tree, and Ed grabbed the chainsaw as he headed in their direction. He jerked the pull cord as he ran, and the saw roared to life. The bear stopped at the base of the tree and turned toward Ed. Ed slowed to a walk as he continued toward the bear. Ed kept pulling the throttle as he approached the bear. The roaring of the engine did the trick, and the bear ran off.

David was shaking when he climbed down from the tree. Ed shut off the chainsaw and turned to David.

"Did you even read the bear-training guide for this job?" Ed asked. "That was a black bear, and black bears can climb trees. You would have been his lunch. Climbing trees will only help you when an adult grizzly is chasing you. They're too heavy to climb."

David's voice quivered as he spoke. "I thought that material was a waste of time."

"Well, you know," Ed replied, "you may consider there are reasons why people tell you something. They have been there before and are trying to help you avoid the same mistakes they made. Only a fool doesn't learn from others and must make all the mistakes on his own. And nature isn't forgiving. If you make just one mistake, it could be your last."

David said nothing for a moment, and when he did, he spoke quietly. "Maybe it would be better if I stayed and helped. Then we could hike out together."

Ed smiled. He knew David had learned another valuable lesson, and there was no use saying more.

The Undesirable Assignment

(Part 3)

Ed worked for a national park in the summers. One summer, he was assigned to have the park superintendent's son, David, work with him. On the first job, deep in the woods, David had not brought the food he was told to take, so Ed had to share his, and they were both hungry. David had decided he was through with all of it, but when he headed back on his own, Ed had to come to David's rescue to save him from a bear.

Ed was pleased that David got in and worked after that. David wanted to return to the main camp, and because of the bear, he didn't dare go alone. The sooner they finished their assignment, the sooner they could head back. Ed had figured it would take four long days to clear the appointed trail, but with David now working hard, they finished by mid-afternoon on the third day. They packed up and headed back.

It had taken them four days to hike in since David had hiked slowly and complained a lot. Ed was a strong hiker and pushed hard despite carrying the heaviest items. Now, desiring to get back, David was keeping up with Ed. But there were still times David complained about the distance.

They had barely started hiking on the morning of the last day heading back, when Ed realized David wasn't with him. Ed followed the trail back to the start of where, for over a quarter mile, it made a u-shape around a murky slough. From that point, the other segment of the trail could be seen about a hundred yards straight across the bog. A dreaded thought came to Ed about where David might have gone, and just as he turned to look across the mire, he heard David scream for help.

Sure enough, David had apparently seen the trail across the

way and, ignoring the warning sign, cut through the quagmire as a shortcut.

Ed went to the edge of the mud. "David, what are you doing? Didn't you see the sign warning of quicksand?"

"I saw it, but I thought if I went fast enough, I could get across without sinking. Help me get out!"

David was almost halfway across, too far to get anything to him from either side. The quicksand was already up to his knees. Ed knew this was a precarious situation.

"David, you're too far out for me to get anything to you. The only way to save you is for you to trust me, and for you to do what I tell you to do."

With fear making his voice tremble, David nodded and said, "I will."

"All right," Ed said, trying to remain calm to help David do the same, "the first thing I need you to do is to drop your pack. Just let it fall into the mud." David did as he was told. "Okay. Now you need to lean back and lay on the mud, gradually working your legs up and out."

"Are you crazy!?" David yelled. "I'll just drown faster!"

"Look," Ed said, "you said you'd trust me. Quicksand is just like thick water. You can't make your way across water standing up. You've got to spread as much of your body on top of the surface as you can so you don't sink."

David paused a moment, and Ed could sense David's fear. Ed saw the pack, which was already starting to sink, and had an idea.

"David, lie down with your back on the pack."

David did that, and the pack sank faster.

"Spread your arms on the surface and start working your legs out carefully," Ed called.

David did as he was told, and his legs were soon on the surface.

"Now," Ed said, "you can't swim out, like in water, so you need to roll out. Just roll across the mud toward me, keeping as much of your body flat on the surface as possible."

David paused briefly, but then did a roll. Then he did another, and another. As soon as David was near enough, Ed reached down, grabbed David by the hand, and pulled him up onto the bank. David continued to tremble as Ed helped him to a stream to wash. When he finished, David didn't look at Ed as he spoke.

"Aren't you going to scold me for not obeying the sign?"

"I think you've already learned your lesson," Ed said.

David nodded. "And I learned to trust someone who has more experience than I do."

And as they walked back to base camp, David didn't complain once about the long trail.

The Undesirable Assignment

(Final)

Ed worked for a national park in the summers. One summer, when he was twenty-one, he was assigned to have the park superintendent's son, David, a rebellious seventeen-year-old, work with him. On the first job, David brought little food, so Ed had to share his, and they were both hungry. Ed saved David from a bear and quicksand because David refused to pay attention to what he was told.

After almost two weeks of working in the backcountry, they were both hungry, and David was much more humble. The first thing they did when they returned to base camp was to have a good meal.

David seemed deep in thought as they ate, but finally, he spoke. "Ed, how did you learn to survive in the backcountry? How did you know about bears, quicksand, and everything?"

"I read the training manuals thoroughly," Ed replied. "But no manual can totally replace experience. Some of that came from my own years growing up on a farm, along with camping, fishing, and hiking. But I also spent some time asking those who had worked here for a while about their experiences."

David said nothing for the rest of the meal. When they finished eating, Ed headed to the main office to complete a report on the work they had done, and David headed to see his father. Ed wondered if he would ever see David again. Ed figured David would tell his father he was through with the hard work and danger of the backwoods. Ed also wondered if David would complain about him and how tough he had been on him.

Ed filled out the paperwork and had a couple of days off. When he returned for his next assignment, his supervisor handed him the paper with his next task. Ed wasn't surprised to see nothing about David working with him. When Ed looked up, his supervisor seemed to know what he was thinking.

"David won't be joining you on this trip."

"Is he done working here?" Ed asked.

His supervisor shrugged. "All I know is his father, the superintendent, said David wouldn't be available. I don't know if that is for now or for good. I figure it will be the latter. I don't think David is really cut out for this."

The next job took Ed over a week to complete. He took his days off and then reported for his next assignment. To his surprise, the paper showed that David would join him. The shock must have shown on his face because when he looked up, his supervisor smiled.

"David's waiting for you at the supply building."

When Ed got to the supply building, David had already packed his pack. He turned to Ed and smiled.

"Go through the checklist of things I should have," David said. "I don't want to forget anything."

Ed packed his own pack as he went through the list, from food to bedding to work equipment. David had almost all of them. There were only two minor items that David needed to add.

As they hiked into the woods to their next job, curiosity was eating at Ed. Finally, he could keep it in no longer. "I thought that when you didn't come back to work on the last assignment, you had quit working here."

David laughed. "You know, if I were the same person who came here a month ago, that would have been true. But those days with you in the backwoods, with your ability to save me from my stupid mistakes, made me think."

"So why didn't you join me on the last job?" Ed asked.

"I needed time to learn," David replied. "I spent that week thoroughly reading the training manual—twice, to be exact. I then asked those who were well seasoned in this work about their experiences. Now I am ready to learn from you, and I hope I won't be as much trouble for you."

Ed was amazed at the change. And the rest of the summer they spent together was much better. There were still some tough times, but David was willing to learn.

As the summer ended, and Ed and David shook hands to go their separate ways, Ed thought that maybe he had just shaken the hand of a future park superintendent.

Ed smiled at the thought because he knew David would be a good one.

Painting the House

There are only a couple of jobs that I really hate to do, and I have been working on one of them this month. I am getting old enough so that I don't brand cattle anymore, so I was doing the other job I hate—painting the house.

When my wife, Donna, suggested we paint the house before winter, my heart filled with a dreaded feeling similar to when I was going in for a root canal. But I couldn't argue that the house needed it. It had been around twenty years since we did it the last time. But the memory of feeling slimy and walking around looking like I had a severe case of yellow measles was as clear as if it had happened yesterday.

And it's not just the gooey mess I hate. I don't like painting from the very start where we have to pick the color. Maybe it's a guy thing, or maybe it's just me, but I like what I am used to. Our house has been a light yellow that has faded to cream, so when Donna asked me what color we should paint the house, I suggested that was the perfect color.

"Oh, no," she said. "We've had it that color for twenty years. It's time we tried something different."

"What color were you thinking?" I asked.

"I was thinking of a tan color," she replied. "That seems to be the color most people are going with these days."

"Well, just because all the other lemmings are jumping off the cliff. . ."

"Oh, stop," she said. "Have you considered that maybe people are painting their houses that color because it is a nice, calming earth tone that is just right for these turbulent days of chaos?"

Painting is not a nice, calming anything for me, and I suggested that if we painted it the same color it already was because if we missed a spot, no one would even know. Her only answer to that was to point out to me all the houses we passed that were tan.

I had to admit they looked quite nice, so the next step was to get the little flip card pack with all the colors. We looked at the tans and finally settled on one. It was called "sand dune," which was ironic since we live close to the famous St. Anthony sand dunes.

"Maybe if the wind picks up, and our house is buried by the blowing sand, no one will even notice," I said.

Next came purchasing the paint. The girl at the paint store asked me what kind of paint I wanted. I told her I wanted the least expensive kind that would last until after I died so I wouldn't have to paint again.

"I don't think we have any that will last that long," she said.

"How young do you think I am?" I asked.

She smiled. "Twenty-nine."

I thought, "Boy, she's good." She could have said, "Five-year paint should do it," but instead, she turned it into a compliment. Her boss needs to give her a raise.

Donna and I settled on the best paint they had so it would last as long as possible, and we set to work. Now, there are some things about painting that are quite illogical. Take the primer, for instance. Why should a person have to paint the house to prepare the house for painting? At least, that's what it seems like to me. It's like eating dinner in preparation for eating dinner. Why don't they just make the paint out of the primer?

Then there was the caulking before I could paint. No one who is a cake decorator should ever be in charge of caulking. Not that I'm a cake decorator. But when I am in charge of making a cake, it's a stack of Twinkies and Ding-Dongs with Cool Whip frosting. It's too tempting to lick your fingers, and unfortunately, caulk looks a lot like Cool Whip. Take it from me, though, it doesn't taste like Cool Whip.

So, we are now about half done, and Donna asked if I like it. Of course, I'm not going to say no for fear I might have to repaint it. But I don't want to lie, either.

I'm sure in about a year, when the painting is done and I am used to it, I will think it is the perfect color.

Stress Reliever

When I was young, my mother made me weed garden rows every summer. My parents also assigned me to help my grandmother in her garden. By the time I left home, I was sure I wouldn't ever want to plant a garden again.

But time changed me. Instead of seeing the garden as a chore, I began to see it differently. One new way I saw it was as a stress reliever. My students struggle with the Covid virus, and I do, too. But if I can get out in the garden and work, I usually feel better. Much of that attitude started while I was working on my master's degree.

My wife, Donna, and I had two little girls at that time. I was working lots of jobs to make ends meet, and stress was building in my life. I felt I needed an outlet.

As spring came, I looked out the back window of our apartment and saw a giant weed patch beyond the parking lot. I called the apartment owners and asked if they would mind if I put a garden in a part of it.

The owner laughed. "Put a garden in all of it if you want. I'd be happy to get rid of the weeds."

I priced the rental of a tiller, and it was out of my budget. I checked at the local farm store and found they had garden forks for only a few dollars, so I bought one and started turning the soil one fork full at a time. I thought I'd only do about a ten-foot by ten-foot spot. But each night when I came home, I would go out and work on the garden, releasing the stress that had built during the day from my math classes, and the garden spot continued to grow.

I would jab the fork forcefully into the ground, turn up the dark soil, and shake the dirt from the weeds before throwing them into a pile. With each fork full of dirt, I felt a little more of the stress leaving me. With nightly frosts, it was too cold to plant most things, so I just kept working the soil. As I did, the children from the apartments came out to watch me work.

"What are you doing?" one boy asked one evening.

"Planting a garden," I replied.

"How big of a garden are you going to plant?" he asked.

"I don't know. I planned to do a small one, but I keep making it bigger."

Little Suzanne joined the conversation. "My momma said you were crazy. My daddy said you weren't crazy, just strange. So they said I could come watch you."

"I might be strange," I said, "but I find working the soil helps relieve stress."

"Can I try?" a boy asked.

I showed him how to use the fork, and he turned over some dirt. Then all the other children wanted a turn. I let each of them try, and they kept asking for another chance until their parents called them in. I worked a while longer, unhindered, then I, too, went in for the night.

"Mrs. Hampton asked how big of a garden you planned to put in," Donna said. "I told her you had only planned to do a small spot, but you kept doing more to relieve stress. She said she hopes you get the stress all worked out before you run out of garden spot and start forking up the parking lot."

We both laughed, but the events of the evening helped me realize how strange I must seem to all the others in the apartment complex. In the next few evenings, I finished up the whole weed area, a spot probably forty feet by thirty feet. My small audience of children continued to watch me and ask for turns to help.

"Why do you want to plant a garden?" one little girl asked.

"I love fresh fruits and vegetables," I replied.

A little boy wrinkled his nose. "I don't like vegetables. The only things I like from gardens are peas and corn."

I smiled. "Have any of you ever grown a garden?"

They all shook their heads.

And that night, as I finished turning up the last of the soil, I had a new purpose. I was not going to just do a garden for my family, but I was going to let all the children experience it.

Gardening With Children

To relieve stress while I was working on my master's degree, I put a garden in where an old weed patch had been behind our apartment complex. I used a garden fork and turned the soil over by hand. When the curious children kept gathering around, I let them be part of it.

When I started planting, the children came to watch and wanted to help. With the younger children, calling it "help" was a misuse of the English language. I learned not to let them plant small things like carrot seeds. They would use an entire bag in about one foot of the row when it should have planted about thirty feet.

I also realized that if I wanted to keep any of the garden produce for my family, I would have to have a segment for the children, and another segment that was mine. I marked off the two areas, separated by a line of twine. I bought the seeds and helped the children plant their section. After work, I came out and saw children standing in the middle of their garden area.

"How come nothing has come up yet?" Suzanne asked. She was an impatient five-year-old.

"It takes some time," I replied. "We only planted it yesterday."

"How much time?" seven-year-old Timothy asked.

"You should probably see the radishes within about two weeks. The other things will take longer."

"Two weeks?" Jordan exclaimed. "That's, like, forever!" Jordan was nine.

"Nothing is going to grow if you keep tromping on it. How would you like somebody standing on your head? You need to look from the edge until the rows come up so you can see where to step."

They all left their garden and came over to watch me. They wanted to help plant mine, but I told them I wanted to do it myself on this part.

"But I have a surprise for you," I said. "You can help me with that when I'm done here."

They were so excited they could hardly stand still. They kept coming into my garden area and tromping my seeded area, so I finally gave up. There were about ten of them, the oldest ones being about twelve years old.

I took the children over to a weed patch at one corner of the lawn. There I had stacked six two-inch by two-inch boards that were each eight feet long. I also had some twine. I had gotten all of it from the scrap pile where I took care of horses.

"What are these for?" Jan, one of the twelve-year-olds, asked.

"We are going to make a fort," I replied. I thought the older children might think that was childish, but even they seemed excited.

First, I dug a square, eight feet on each side. Then, after moving the children out of the way, I took an ax and sharpened the boards to a point on one end. Next, I pounded one board into the ground at each corner of the square. Lastly, I pounded in the last two boards two feet apart in the middle of the side by the lawn. That would be the door.

The children kept asking questions about what I was doing, and I just kept telling them to wait and see. Once the boards were in place, I gave each of the children some twine to untangle. Then we started tying strands between the boards on each side at about six-inch intervals, all the way to the top. We left the lowest four feet of the door area uncovered.

When we finished the twine, Jan said, "It's not much of a fort."

"There's one more thing," I replied.

I gave each child a handful of climbing beans and showed them how to plant them about four inches apart along the sides, except in the doorway. The older children helped the younger ones.

They all looked skeptical when we finished. I could see they struggled to envision it, but their curiosity and excitement were unbounded. The only thing that was greater was their impatience.

I just hoped I could get them to leave the seeds alone long enough for the plants to grow.

Something New and Better

The children who had watched me work in the garden impatiently waited for the plants to come up in the section I set aside for them. I knew something must be up when I came home from work, and they were all waiting for me.

"Jordan found some stuff growing in our garden," five-year-old Suzanne said.

They all nodded their agreement. I dropped my books off in my apartment and followed the children out to the garden. Jordan proudly showed me his discovery.

"I hate to tell you this," I said, "but those are weeds. We can't pull them yet, or we will hurt the baby plants that are growing under the ground." I then suggested we check on the radishes since they're the first non-weed plants to germinate. I led the way there and knelt down. The children knelt beside me.

"If you look at those tiny little green leaves, those are radishes," I said, pointing to the small plants.

The children chattered with excitement. And over the next few weeks, their excitement grew as other things came up. When the first pea pods began to show, it was all I could do to get the children to wait until the peas had grown inside. But finally, the day came when there was enough for each child to have one.

When I told the children it was time to try the peas, even some of the more skeptical teenagers followed us out to the garden. I showed the children what to look for and how to pick the peas without pulling the plant out by the roots. Their eyes appeared full of wonder at what they had helped grow. As I passed peas out to everyone, Sam, the oldest teenager, shook his head.

"Nah. I hate peas."

I laughed. "If you haven't tried one fresh out of the garden, you have a surprise coming. These and the frozen or canned ones from the store aren't even in the same pod."

Most of the children didn't get my joke, but Sam did and rolled his eyes. Still, he took the full pea pod from me. I then showed the children how to run their fingers along the pod to open it without smashing the valuable little green pearls inside. The younger children laughed as they opened theirs. They all smiled with delight as they each tried it. Sam's eyes lit up when he got a taste.

"Those are really fantastic!" he exclaimed.

I was able to find another one for each child, and we agreed to come out together each night so they could all share equally. I then took my little entourage over to look at the climbing bean fort. The vines were already halfway up the poles and twine and had tiny beans on them. The children were starting to get the vision of what it would be.

I shared a lot of trips to the garden with the children that summer. I taught them to weed, and they found it exciting, a feeling I encouraged while it lasted. We could have always used more vegetables, though there was much more for everyone. Some, like Sam, would sneak out and get some when they thought others wouldn't see them. They were afraid of being called childish. Many of the children started taking their portion home to share with their families. I shared a lot from my part of the garden with the others, too.

One day, as we were dividing up the produce, the topic turned to when I had first started turning the soil over one fork full at a time. "Do your parents still think I'm crazy?"

"No," Suzanne said. "Momma now agrees with daddy that you're just strange, but she says it's a good strange."

Fall frosts eventually came, and the children were sad to see the garden turn brown and stop producing. The next spring, I finished my degree, and I wondered if anyone would be interested in the garden. None of the adults seemed to be. But I couldn't just leave it. I paid a man to come till it the day before I left.

After packing the last things in the truck, I looked out the window at the garden and saw it all subdivided with twine. Each family had a portion, and the children were busy showing their parents how to plant vegetables. The children all seemed so happy and proud of themselves.

Maybe what I taught the children was more than just how to grow a garden.

A Privy Halloween Operation

The five friends gathered for lunch at their regular spot in the old high school. They always ate together, but Halloween was only a few days away, and they were meeting to plan their activities. Matthew spoke first.

"You know, with so many of the young men away for the war, we really need to step up our game. Anyone have any ideas?"

"What would they do if they were here?" Susan asked.

"My older brother, who's fighting the Nazis in Europe, used to always tip over outhouses," Elizabeth replied.

"Then we should do it for him," Matthew said.

"What if we get caught?" Alice asked.

Matthew laughed. "We're too good. We never get caught."

"Doing the same thing others have done is no fun," Clarence said. "Maybe we need to do something more."

"Like what?" Susan asked.

"If we just tip over the outhouse," Clarence replied, "then the person can just lift it back up. But if we carried it a distance away, they would have to get help to carry it back. That would mean they would probably have to use the uncovered latrine for a while."

Everyone laughed at the thought of someone sitting in an open privy. They all agreed that Clarence's idea was the thing to do. And for the next couple of days, they talked about it.

On Halloween night, they met at Matthew's house. It was the perfect evening, with the clouds ominously covering the moon, with only slightly shadowy light breaking through. The group tipped over a few outhouses around town, but they couldn't carry them very far in the small yards. They almost got caught once when a dog sounded the alarm, but they all ran fast and got away.

They then decided to move out into the country, so they piled into Matthew's Studebaker. After tipping over the first country outhouse, they took positions along the sides and carried it a distance away like a coffin. They hit a few more, and then it was Clarence's turn to choose.

"I know just the outhouse," Clarence said. "The old guy that lives close to us is the grouchiest man alive."

Clarence gave them directions, and they soon pulled up to a long lane that led to the farmhouse. They decided they had better park the car on the road and walk from there. They made their way to the house, with Clarence leading the way. There was barely enough moonlight to avoid obstacles. They circled wide around the house to the backyard, tipped over the outhouse, and stealthily carried it around to the side of the barn.

They were chuckling about their misdeed as they circled around the house toward the car. They were just passing the house when the front door burst open, and the farmer came flying out with a baseball bat in his hand. He ran straight toward them, and there was nothing they could do but head back toward the barn.

With Clarence leading the way at breakneck speed, they ran around the back of the house and out into the pasture. When they were quite a distance from the farmhouse, they turned toward the road. It was then that they realized someone was missing. It was Alice.

"I know she was close to us up to the time we ran past the hole where the outhouse had been," Elizabeth said.

No one had seen her past that point, and it quickly dawned on them what had probably happened to her. They hurried back, and by the time they got to the scene of the crime, the farmer was already fishing Alice out of the outhouse pit. Soon, Alice was standing, shivering, by the rest of them.

They knew they were caught. The farmer took them to his house, and his wife had Alice wash, then she gave her some dry clothes. The farmer summoned their parents. As punishment, the group had to set up the outhouse of anyone who had had theirs tipped over, even the ones their group hadn't hit. It took them two full evenings, with the people smirking as they watched. Matthew said he thought some people tipped over their own outhouses just so they could laugh while the group set it back up.

Alice didn't say too much as they went around and did their assignment. The odor of her ordeal still lingered with her. But when they finished the last outhouse, she finally spoke.

"Guys, I think if you decide to tip over outhouses next year, I might just stay home and read a book."

Senior Hour

Have you ever had what you considered was a good idea, only to have it backfire? A case in point is something that happened recently because of the Covid virus.

Many stores tried having what they called Senior Hour when only senior citizens could come into the store. The idea was that the seniors would stay away from everyone else and not bring the sickness back to their homes. Also, a critical part of the thinking was that by not allowing anyone else in, the numbers would be reduced, and there would be a natural form of social distancing.

In the beginning days of the virus, I saw many big box stores announce that they would do this. I am about to the age I could qualify, but I hate to think of myself as a senior citizen. So, I just took my chances with everyone else.

Many points of failure were built into this supposedly good idea. First, many stores had their senior hour before or after regular open times. This meant it was either after many senior citizens had gone to bed or before they got up. I'm sure there are a few seniors it worked for. My mother would be one. She has called me at four in the morning, still stuck in the schedule from when we had cows to milk. But for many, it just wasn't convenient.

Still, with the stores trying to help protect their senior customers, I couldn't fault them for trying. But two other issues ended up being even more of a problem.

The first issue was that some stores advertised it so heavily that many senior citizens thought they were no longer allowed to shop during regular hours. I know some who got up early or stayed up late just because they thought they would be turned away if they went at standard times. This information made some stores fuller during the senior hour than during the regular times of the day.

But the biggest issue was the lack of foresight this policy had in specific communities, especially combined with some seniors' idea that they had to go during that time.

My sister-in-law, Tammy, moved in with her father to help take care of him. He had previously moved to a community that was almost all senior citizens. When a big store chain announced that all their stores nationwide would have a senior hour early in the morning, it was big news in that community. There were lots of advertisements, much discussion on social media, and talk about it all over town.

Tammy's father suggested that she go shopping at that time. She was old enough to qualify. She also considered that it might help her avoid bringing anything home to him. So, when she needed to make a grocery run, she got up early and made the trek to the store. What she found was not convenience nor social distancing, but rather, pure chaos.

Since almost everyone in the community was a senior citizen, most of the citizens were there. There were so many people that there was hardly a square foot of the store that didn't have someone already standing in it. Social distancing was impossible. And the lines were clear to the back of the store. Everyone was irritable from getting up early, and the overworked store clerks were not happy.

Tammy decided to turn around and go home. Later in the day, during regular hours, she went back to the store. There were so few cars in the parking lot that she almost wondered if the store was closed. But it was open, and virtually no one was there. She quickly got everything she needed and went to check out. There were no lines, and some clerks were even waiting for customers to come to their stands.

As she was checking out, Tammy told the clerk about her experience earlier that morning. The clerk nodded.

"In this community, it shouldn't be senior hour—it should be senior day. Every day."

Curious Grandchildren

I have the smartest grandchildren. Of course, all grandparents think they do, but I really do. My daughter and her family came to spend a few weeks with us in the summer, and I quickly learned how smart my grandchildren are. Of course, part of intelligence is a matter of curiosity, and it wasn't long before I learned how curious a two-year-old girl and a three-year-old boy can be.

Because of the Covid virus, I'm teaching from home. I'd love to be in the classroom with my students, but there are no good options for that. So I have a section of my house set up with a whiteboard, a camera, and all my teaching station necessities.

The problem with all those things is that they are nothing but an endless supply of items for children to explore. And so, soon after they came, I had a day of teaching that went something like this:

After verbally explaining the material using PowerPoint slides, I went to a slide with a sample question.

"All right, everyone," I said, "go ahead and punch these numbers into your calculator, and I will do the same."

At that point, I reached for my calculator, but it was nowhere to be seen. That was when I remembered my granddaughter watching me while I used it, and I was sure I knew why I couldn't find it. So I said, "I will also punch it in the minute I find out what my granddaughter has done with my calculator."

I then tried to do a quick search for the calculator but had no luck. I have a big box of dollar store calculators I bought to share with my students in the classroom. So instead of my one-hundred-and-fifty-dollar calculator, I grabbed a dollar store one. The buttons were small and hard to punch, but my class was waiting.

At that point, I returned to my computer and said, "Okay, I found a calculator. Does anyone already have the answer?"

Inevitably, by that point, someone did. A student shared her answer with all of us. "That looks good," I said. "Now, let's talk in more depth about this answer as I write it on my whiteboard."

At that point, I reached for my whiteboard markers and found every one of them was missing its cap. I tried to write with some of them, but they wrote so lightly that they were impossible to see on the computer screen.

"Okay," I said, "I will be right back after I go get a new marker."

Luckily, I had a cupboard with a stash of new markers. I went and retrieved a couple and took them to my teaching station. I switched to the whiteboard camera and wrote the problem on the board. When I turned to look at my computer screen, it showed an image of one of my ceiling lights. That was when I remembered my grandson asking me what the camera attached to my desk was for. He must have turned it.

My students hadn't even said anything while I was writing the problem. It made me wonder if any of them were really with me in the discussion. But I got the camera facing the whiteboard, and we discussed the problem. Things did go better after that. But when I looked to check the clock to see how much time I had left for class, I found it was missing.

As you can imagine, every day after that, before it was time for class to start, I tried to check and make sure everything was ready. I could no longer assume anything would be in the place I put it the last time I used it. I also put a box of markers and dollar store calculators on a shelf, supposedly out of the reach of children. I say "supposedly" because I was continually surprised at what they could get into.

That evening, the children came to sit by me after their baths, and my granddaughter asked, "Gampa, can we watch a kitty movie on ootube?"

I found a good one, and they snuggled up close as we all watched it on my small computer screen. And even after all the craziness of the day, I smiled and thought, "Thank heaven for sweet, darling grandchildren."

A Difference in Age

Lindy and her husband, Kevin, were new to our community. Donna, my wife, wanted to get to know them and welcome them in. She made a batch of brownies, and in the evening, we made our way to their house to deliver them. Lindy met us at the door and invited us in.

Lindy was a boisterous young lady, and she did almost all the talking for both of them. After we settled on the couch across from them, I asked Kevin what he did for a living. Before he could answer, Lindy did.

"Kevin is into construction. He works mostly as a manual laborer, but he is hoping to eventually get a certificate as a plumber."

"That sounds good," I replied. "Have you heard the joke about the surgeon and the plumber?"

They shook their heads.

"Well, a plumber did some work on a surgeon's house, and when he finished, he gave the surgeon the bill. When the surgeon looked at it, he gasped. 'Why, I don't even make this amount per hour, and I'm a surgeon.' The plumber nodded. 'You know, when I was a surgeon, I didn't either,' he said."

They laughed, and Lindy said, "We hope he makes good money." She then turned to me. "So, what do you do for a living?"

"I am a professor at Ricks College," I replied.

"What do you teach?"

"I teach math."

Lindy wrinkled her nose. "I can't believe anybody likes math. I'm sure it's an old person thing. Today, with calculators and everything, who needs it?" Lindy then turned to Donna and asked, "Do you like math?"

Donna shrugged. "I like it okay, but I'm not into it as much as Daris is."

It was Donna's turn to ask a get-to-know-you question. Her favorite topic when meeting other married couples is to find out how they met. It almost always leads to something interesting. So that's what she asked.

"Oh, that's really fun," Lindy said. "I was working at a fast-food restaurant taking orders when a whole group of guys from his construction crew came in. When they ordered, Kevin smiled at me, and I just felt my heart melt. The others must have seen it. They challenged him to ask me out. Kevin is rather shy and wasn't going to, but one guy said he would lend Kevin his truck for the date. Kevin had always wanted to drive the guy's beautiful pickup, so he decided he would."

Lindy went on to tell us about how Kevin came and asked her. She talked about their first date and some of the crazy things they did, as well as some about other dates. She finished by saying, "And, well, here we are."

Lindy then asked, "So, how did you meet?"

"We met at Ricks College," I replied.

"Wow!" Lindy said. "Was she a student in one of your classes? I didn't think you were supposed to date your students."

Donna snickered, and I glanced at her. Lindy must have noticed because she said, "I mean, you know, the age difference and all."

"We were both in school at the time," I replied.

Again, Lindy looked shocked. "You must have gone to school late in life."

I shook my head. "We're only three years different in age."

Once more, Lindy looked surprised, but answered in a sympathetic tone. "I'm sorry. You must have been through a lot in your life."

By this time, Donna was almost choking to keep back her laughter. Kevin looked mortified about what his wife was saying and seemed to want to stop her. He spoke the first words I heard him say all evening.

"Hey, everybody, how about some brownies?"

I nodded. "Sounds good to me."

Hey, I might as well be both old and fat.

Truly a Day of Thanksgiving

It was Thanksgiving, but Aaron struggled to feel thankful. It was 1918, and the hostilities of The Great War had just ended on November eleventh, though the terms of peace were still being negotiated. People were still euphoric about the cessation of fighting. Aaron was also grateful the conflict was over, but that would not bring Sam home. Why couldn't the war have ended just a few months earlier? Then Sam would still be alive.

Aaron could still remember the day two months earlier when they learned Sam was missing in action. His sweet wife, Mary, had just collapsed into a chair and sobbed. The children had all shown the impact of the loss of their brother in different ways. Some cried for days, while others became quiet and solitary.

As much as he wanted to, Aaron couldn't find it in himself to be of any comfort to the others. The loss of his son was such a shock to him that it paralyzed his thoughts and feelings. Additionally, some of the children were still sick with the Spanish flu. Though he felt they were winning on that front, and that the children would pull through, it seemed a daily touch-and-go situation. On top of all of that, they were all under quarantine because of the sickness in their home. Their hope of enjoying the holiday with extended family was impossible.

As Aaron finished milking the cows that morning, he struggled to count his blessings instead of his challenges. Though everyone in the family had gotten sick, his own strength had been sufficient to allow him to continue doing the chores. Most of the family was now well, but he still worried about the three that weren't. Still, his family had enough food so they didn't go hungry, and they even had extra to share with those who were less fortunate. Aaron's thoughts ping-ponged back and forth from blessings to challenges.

Aaron went to the smokehouse and got the turkey he had

prepared for their Thanksgiving meal. It was a big one that he had raised, and it would provide a lot of good food for the family. He took it to the house where his wife was making pies and rolls. Aaron could see her eyes were red and knew she had been crying. Even though losing Sam was hard for her, she always tried to be cheerful.

She forced a smile and asked, "Do you think Alice will make it home for Thanksgiving?"

"I hope so," Aaron said.

Alice had volunteered to work as a nurse during the pandemic. She had been gone for almost four months. The last letter had indicated she had caught the flu, but she was optimistic she would beat it. Since then, they had heard nothing, and Aaron just kept telling himself that no news was good news. Still, there was always the nagging in his mind that something could have gone wrong.

Aaron sat down and started peeling potatoes. Helping prepare the food took his mind off his worries. The wonderful aromas of the cooking food helped lift his spirits—a little. When it was time to eat, Aaron carried each of the sick children to their chairs at the table. But as he looked at the two seats that were still empty, he could no longer bear the pain and walked to his bedroom so his family wouldn't see him cry. He hadn't been there very long when he heard the excited voices of the children.

He returned and saw the reason for their exuberance. Alice was coming up the lane with a stranger. The stranger was on crutches, so their pace was slow. Aaron and Mary rushed out of the house with most of the children close behind. Aaron swooped his daughter into his arms and twirled her around.   When he finally stopped and set her down, she smiled.

"Look who I found at the train station!"

Aaron turned to the stranger, and the man pulled back the hood that covered his face. Aaron gasped to see Sam standing there. He was missing an arm and a leg, and his face was scarred, but it was him.

Tears poured down Aaron's face—not tears of sadness, but tears of joy. He pulled his son into an embrace Aaron would remember for the rest of his life.

As the family gathered around the table with every seat filled, gratitude filled Aaron's heart, and the challenges of that time faded away. The joy of being together as a family once more outshone everything else.

It truly was a day of Thanksgiving.

Disqualified

It was the early 1980s, and the International Olympic Committee had been doing drug testing for some time. Though the National College Athletic Association hadn't yet implemented similar measures, there was talk of it possibly coming. It was against this backdrop that Martin walked into the college wrestling room and handed me a news article, saying, "Hey, Howard, you've got to read this."

We were warming up but hadn't yet started practice, and since Coach wasn't there, I sat down to read. I had just begun when Coach walked in.

"Howard, are you too good to join us for warm-ups?"

"Sorry, Coach," I replied. "Martin just handed me something to read."

"What's it about?" Coach asked.

Martin laughed. "Oh, you would love it. It's about an athlete that had some problems with drug testing."

"Well, maybe we should all hear it," Coach said. "Howard, read it out loud."

All the wrestlers gathered around and sat cross-legged on the mat, and I started to read.

The article was about athletes on a team that had come under suspicion of drug use, causing the entire team to face suspension. To avoid such a severe penalty, the coach cut a deal allowing an independent doctor to test the athletes for drugs. Only the athletes who tested positive would be suspended from the team, and the rest could finish out the season. The coach agreed to live by whatever decision the doctor made.

However, when the doctor's list was posted, the star athlete's name was flagged for drug use. The athlete was livid. He said he knew for sure that there was no way his urine sample could have had drugs in it. The coach, taking the side of the athlete, insisted on a hearing, demanding that the doctor explain his reasoning on the matter.

The doctor agreed, and a formal hearing board was convened to determine whether the doctor's decision would be upheld. After the hearing started, the athlete was given the floor. He insisted he had the highest character and knew his urine sample could not have had any drugs in it. He went so far as to claim his suspension could be nothing more than prejudice on the part of the doctor.

The coach was then given a chance to speak. He expounded on this great athlete's virtues, claiming he knew the athlete had the highest moral values, both in competition and in life. The coach said that is why he had called for the hearing. He said he knew something had to be wrong with the doctor's judgment in the matter. He even said he felt the doctor was possibly guilty of malpractice.

Finally, it was the doctor's turn. When the board members asked the doctor what drug or drugs he had found in the athlete's urine sample, the doctor said he hadn't found any.

"Then why in heaven's name did you suspend him from competition?" the coach demanded.

"Because," the doctor said, "he has a condition that makes competing somewhat impossible for the rest of the athletic season."

"And just what condition would that be?" a board member asked.

The doctor turned to look directly at the athlete and the coach as he replied. "He is pregnant." Everyone in the room seemed stunned by the revelation as the doctor continued. "I realized, of course, it couldn't have really been his urine used for the sample. I debated disqualifying him from any further competition for cheating on the drug test, but I decided instead to only disqualify him for the rest of the season for pregnancy. If the coach would prefer, we can switch it to a permanent disqualification."

At that point, the coach and the athlete chose to withdraw their disputation of the doctor's decision. And that is how a male athlete was disqualified from competition because of pregnancy.

When I finished reading the article, Martin laughed and turned to Coach. "Hey, Coach, if one of us did that, would it disqualify us from competing?"

"If you put me in a situation like that," Coach growled, "when I got hold of you, you would be disqualified from living."

A Little Absent Minded

When we visit our children, one thing I really enjoy is a pizza and movie night with my grandchildren. It usually gives their parents time for a date, and it gives my wife and me time with our grandchildren. I always buy the pizza and the pop and rent the movie.

One time, we were visiting our daughter, Celese, and her family in California. When it came time to get the pizza and the movie, I asked the grandchildren what they wanted to watch. They settled on Veggie Tales. Frankly, I didn't know what Veggie Tales was, but I was more concerned about time with them than I was about the type of movie, as long as it was kid-friendly.

I invited my grandchildren to go with me to pick it out, and they gladly headed out to the van. Then, since I was unfamiliar with the city and didn't have a GPS, I asked Celese for directions to the nearest video store.

"Hey, Dad, why don't I just go with you?" she replied. "That would be easier than trying to tell you how to get there."

Since I am very much a country person, I think she was afraid I would get lost with her children, and she would never see them again. But having her go sounded like a good idea.

We all piled into the van and headed on our way. We wound all over the place and finally came to a stop in front of a huge grocery store. We trouped in and went directly to the video rental. The children picked out a video, handed it to me, and then followed me to the front of the store so I could pay for the rental. We then all went out and climbed back in the van.

After everyone was buckled, I turned to Celese and asked, "Now, where do we go for pizza?"

"Oh," she said, "this place has got the best pizza. They make a take-n-bake pizza that is fabulous. We can just buy it here."

So, we all unloaded out of the van again and went to the pizza counter. After we decided what we wanted, I ordered it. We waited until it was ready, then we traipsed back to the front to pay for it. It just happened that the shortest line was with the same lady that had been the checker for the video.

"Back again so soon?" she asked.

I nodded. "Yeah, we didn't get the pizza."

I paid for the pizza, and we all loaded into the van again. We had just finished buckling again when one child asked, "Grandpa, weren't you going to get some pop?"

"Yes," I said. "I totally forgot that."

The children were tired of going in and out of the store, so they just told me the kinds of pop they wanted, and then they stayed in the van.

Celese went with me. "There are a few things I need to get," she said. "I will just find them while you get the pop."

"Do you want me to wait for you?" I asked.

She shook her head. "You go ahead and check out. I'll take care of my own stuff."

I found the pop and selected the kinds the children wanted, along with root beer for me. When I went to check out, I had hoped to find someone new, but the same clerk as before was the only one with no one in her checkout line.

She looked at me with a strange look as I rolled my cart up. "Just forgot the pop," I said. I joked about it and said, "This is the last thing I forgot. I promise."

After I finished paying for it, I quickly left the store. But as I was putting the pop from the cart into the van, I realized I was missing the case of root beer that I had paid for. Just then, Celese came out pushing her cart, sporting a grin.

"Dad, did you forget anything else?" she asked.

I nodded. "I forgot the root beer, and with the way the lady looked at me last time, I think I will just leave it here."

Celese laughed, pulled the root beer from her cart, and said, "The lady handed this to me on my way out and asked if you were my father. When I said yes, she laughed and said, 'Well, it looks like you turned out okay, anyway.'"

41

Zooming

The world of Zoom is interesting. Being in education, I have had a fair amount of training on Zoom. Some of that training has centered around what happens if someone hacks or bombs your Zoom session. I was grateful a couple of weeks ago for that training.

It's hard to believe that someone, or a group of people, can find great joy in creating havoc. I had heard of Zoom bombing, but it was hard to envision it. But my cousin asked me to be the technical person for an online book group meeting. We were only about a half-hour into the discussion when we were bombed.

It was not just one person. It was a coordinated attack by many people. As soon as I removed someone, they would come back in with a different account. I locked down the session and removed people as fast as I could. It was probably only a couple of minutes, but it seemed like it was twenty. All the training in the world doesn't quite compare to the real thing when your session is under attack. I guess it's kind of like the difference between boot camp and actual battle in a minimal way.

But on the lighter side of Zoom sessions, I have had some funny things happen that others might have experienced as well. I thought I'd share some of them.

The standard protocol for students is to keep their microphones off unless they are speaking. Most of the time, a student will hold the spacebar as they talk. When they release it, their microphone goes back to mute. If a student wants to speak for quite a while, they will hit the unmute button. But then they must remember to mute their mic when they finish.

One day, I had a student who was asking about a problem from the homework. Since he and I were discussing it back and forth, he had unmuted his microphone. When we finished with his question, he forgot to hit mute again. At that point, he turned, and though you couldn't see anyone else, you could tell he was speaking to a child. He said, "I'm sorry.

Daddy is really busy right now. You will have to wipe your own bummy."

In one class session, one young lady talked on her cell phone the whole time. That class was small enough so she showed on everyone's screen. A person can shut off their video, but apparently she didn't think to do that.

In Zoom, a teacher can have breakout rooms for the students to go into. There the students can discuss the assigned topic. After a given amount of time, the teacher can close the rooms, bringing everyone back together to go over what they discussed. I will often do this, then join each room briefly to see how it was going. When the students or the teacher go into a breakout room, their microphones automatically unmute. In joining one room just after opening them, one girl turned to a roommate and said, "I can't go with you right now. I have to work with these dumb people in this stupid class." After she turned back to her computer, another girl said, "So, us dumb people are ready to start the discussion, are you?"

One person was munching chips and slurping pop in one class, apparently unaware her mic was on. A few people asked her to mute her mic, but she couldn't hear them. Luckily, I was able to do it reasonably fast.

I have had students fall asleep and snore, probably with their hand on the space bar so they pressed down on it as they fell asleep. The problem was I could mute them, but the space bar immediately unmuted them. We eventually got them awake. I have also had roommates of my students walk in the background less than fully clothed.

One of my favorites was a girl who was fishing out on a lake. She had set her computer or phone up on a rock where she could watch and listen to the class discussion while she fished. We even watched her pull in a fish or two during the class period because she didn't realize her video was on. I think the class was more interested in her activities than in my class. That was probably because the rest of us wished we could be fishing, too.

Christmas Change of Heart

Jane hated Christmas, but it hadn't always been that way. When she was young, she looked forward to Christmas and the magic of it. That didn't change when she got married. She had hoped for children, and none came. But then her only child, Jonathan, was born in the Christmas season.

Jonathan brought added magic to her as she saw the wonder in his bright eyes. She loved to shop for that special gift for him and see his excitement when he saw it under the tree. Her husband, Richard, loved Christmas, too. He put up Christmas lights and helped her decorate the tree. He made sure they all watched Christmas movies on TV and made apple cider and hot chocolate.

As much as she loved Christmas, it was also a hectic time. Jonathan always had school Christmas plays and concerts. Jane always felt a need to get out lots of Christmas cards and bake cookies for all of the neighbors. And then, of course, there was the shopping.

But now, Christmas only brought back the memory of that Christmas when she had been overstressed. Jonathan had been away at college and was coming home. She wanted everything to be just right. But instead of making it perfect, when Jonathan came home, she seemed to get annoyed at everything. Just a few days before Christmas, Jonathan did something that made her snap. She yelled at him, and the more he tried to reason with her, the madder she got. Finally, he just walked out the door.

When she calmed down, she set about making cookies and trying to make it nice for when he came back so she could apologize. But he didn't come back—not that night, not for Christmas, not ever. It had been eight years. She hated the Christmas season because it reminded her of Jonathan's birthday and why he was gone. She knew that mainly she hated herself.

Richard still decorated and tried to make Christmas nice, but she wanted nothing to do with it. She knew he was hurting, too, but he never showed it. He always said, "Christmas is about hope. If we lose that, we've lost everything. And I hope Jonathan will come home someday."

Now, here it was Christmas Eve again. Richard said, "There's a beautiful Christmas display I read about. I'm going to go see it. Would you like to come with me?" Jane didn't want to go, but she didn't relish being home alone.

It started snowing as they left, and it was almost an hour's drive to another town through an isolated area. The farmlands and trees looked beautiful covered in white, but Jane struggled to find beauty in anything. The light display was also beautiful, but she pushed Richard to hurry through it, wanting to return home.

On the way back, the storm increased, and in the middle of the farmland, a car was off the road. Richard wanted to stop and see if the people were okay, but Jane vehemently refused. She struggled to feel any love in her heart. "They're probably just out drinking or something," she said. "No decent person would be out in this."

But after Richard got her safely home, he headed back to the car. "Where are you going?" Jane asked.

"I feel a strong need to help those people in that car. I'm heading back."

Jane tried to talk him out of it, saying he would get stuck or something, but he went anyway. As time went by, she grew more and more worried. She should have just let him stop on their way home. She felt relieved when she finally heard Richard's car pull into the driveway.

Richard stomped off the snow as he came in. He smiled at her. "What say we do Christmas tonight? I've got something for you."

Jane sighed. "Richard, I told you not to buy me anything."

His smile widened. "I didn't." He stepped aside, and there

stood Jonathan. When Jonathan stepped into the room, following him came a beautiful woman and two small children.

"They had car trouble on the way here," Richard said.

"I decided Timmy and Lilly needed to meet their grandparents for Christmas," Jonathan said.

Jane sobbed as she ran to her son. He hugged his mother and said, "Dad always said Christmas is about hope. But I've learned it's also about forgiveness."

That night, as Jane made cookies for her grandchildren, she smiled. She was so grateful for the Christmas season—a season of hope and forgiveness.

A Needed/Useful Gift

My mother is almost ninety-five and hard to buy gifts for. She always says, "Don't buy me things. I probably have everything I need, and if I don't, I will get it when I need it."

So, for Christmas, my wife, Donna, suggested we take Mom out for dinner, and that I spend some time doing things Mom wanted to do. So, one evening when Donna had a casting meeting for a play she was directing, we picked up Mom and took her to a buffet restaurant.

We went before the dinner crowd came, so there weren't many people there. There was a large variety of food, and we ate heartily. Sometimes Mom wanted to try something, but not enough to get it, so I would put some on my plate. Then she would take what she wanted and leave me the rest.

This caused some challenges. Sometimes Mom didn't like it after trying it and left me far more than I wanted. I hardly dared not eat it. My parents grew up during the depression, and they taught me to waste nothing. But there were still other foods I wanted to try. By the time we left, I was so full I was almost sick, and I could barely waddle out the door.

On the way out, Mom stopped at the check-in counter and turned to me. "Do you think your brother would like a gift certificate for him and his wife to eat here?"

"Sure, Mom," I replied. "I think he'd love that."

"If you think he'd use it, I'll get him one," she said. "My rule for buying presents is preferably to get something the person needs, and if not, at least something they will use."

I assured her I thought my brother and his wife would use the gift certificate, so she purchased it. Then, while Donna worked on the play casting, I took Mom to see some beautiful light displays. We also enjoyed visiting. Before I took her home for the evening, she said there was one more thing she wanted to do. She doesn't drive much, and she wanted someone to take her shopping for Christmas gifts. So we worked out a time I could take her.

When I picked her up for the shopping trip a few days later, she had two lists. One was of the places she wanted to go, and one had the addresses of my brothers and sisters so she could mail the things she purchased.

Except for one gift, everything she listed for my siblings was a gift certificate to a restaurant. The exception was our first stop, a honey farm. Mom wasn't sure what restaurants existed where my youngest sister lived, so she purchased a bucket of honey and had the store mail it to her. For my other brothers and sisters, Mom named off the restaurant she thought would be their favorites. There was a steakhouse for a brother, a Chinese restaurant for a sister, and so on. Each time she would buy the gift certificate, she would say, "This is something I'm sure they will use." As we continued through the list, I wondered what restaurant she would choose for me. I was curious about which one she thought would be my favorite.

When we finished with all the gift certificates she was buying for my brothers and sisters, it was lunchtime. We went to eat at a place she enjoyed going to with my father before he passed away. It had an all-you-can-eat salad bar with chicken, Mexican food, and many other things besides salad items. We ate our fill, and I got each of us some ice-cream for dessert.

As we were leaving, she mentioned that for me, she had gotten something she thought I needed. That made me even more curious since, for my siblings, she had never talked about the gift as being something they needed, but something they would use. When I took her home, she handed me a gift. When the time came that I opened it, I found it was a book for older people on losing weight and gaining muscle.

I don't think I need to tell you what my New Year's resolution is—let one of my siblings take Mom shopping for Christmas next year.

The Right Clothing

Judy was really sick, and she didn't get better. Finally, her husband, Kent, decided she needed to go to the hospital.

"Let's wait until morning," Judy said. "I'm sure I'll be better by then."

But at four in the morning, Judy woke Kent. "We'd better go now."

Sometime after they got to the emergency room, the word came back, Judy had COVID. She had lots of blood clots in her lungs, and her heart was failing. She was so bad that they decided they needed to transfer her to a larger regional medical center. Kent was told he would not be allowed into the hospital's ICU wing, but they would keep him informed of her condition.

Within a day, her health had deteriorated to the point that the doctor told Kent to call the family together because Judy would not last very long. When word got around our little community, everyone started to pray for Judy. She was not expected to make it through the night. However, she not only made it through the night, but her condition had slightly improved the next morning.

As prayers continued over the next few days, Judy continued to get better. Soon she was moved out of intensive care to another floor of the hospital. Kent finally got word that he would be allowed to visit her. It was a joyous reunion. A couple of days later, she was moved again, and shortly thereafter, she was told she could go home.

Kent was already on his way to visit Judy and got word after he arrived. He was excited to have her come home. But he hadn't known soon enough to bring her any clothes. Her original ones had been left at the first hospital. She had nothing to wear and was not about to go out in an "I See You" hospital gown.

"Kent," she said, "go to Walmart and get me something I can wear home."

"What should I get?" he asked.

"Just a simple muumuu would be good," she replied.

When Kent got to the store, he asked a young teenage clerk where he would find a muumuu.

"I don't think we carry those," she replied.

Kent called Judy and asked her what he should do.

"I'm sure they carry them," she said. "But you need to ask a woman who's over fifty. Any female younger than that, or a man, probably wouldn't know what one is."

Kent found an older clerk, and she told him they did, indeed, carry muumuus. She then directed a teenage girl to show him where they were. Since Kent wasn't sure what a muumuu was, and because the girl was young, he was concerned that the items she showed him might not be right. He debated whether or not to buy one. Then he saw the Halloween clearance aisle.

In it he found a cute, adult, full-length bunny costume. It even had ears and everything. And to clinch the deal, it was on sale for seventy-five percent off since Halloween had been the previous week.

When he brought the bunny costume to the hospital, Judy probably wondered if people would question her sanity if she left the hospital in it. But she wanted to go home, so she donned the suit. There were more than a few smiles as she left. She was probably the first person ever released from the hospital dressed as a bunny.

Kent told this story and a few others. I asked if I could share them with my readers.

"Sure," he said. "If you feel people would like them, go ahead."

I wrote some notes and then went to my wife with a question. "Honey, what is this muumuu thing that Judy wanted Kent to buy for her?"

She looked at my notes and laughed. "A muumuu is just a type of dress that hangs from the shoulders. But I think you might offend some women if you spell it moo moo."

I'm obviously not a woman over fifty.

The Power of a Child

My daughter, Elliana, works at a fast-food restaurant. She says that since the pandemic has started, it seems like people who come in either seem to be nicer than usual or meaner than usual. The challenging times seem to have pushed people toward the extremes.

One day, Elliana was one of the workers on the drive-through headset. A man came through, and he seemed to be in a foul mood. To make matters worse, when he ordered, it was hard to hear him. It sounded like he kept turning away from the speaker.

"Did you say you wanted a large on that?" the worker taking the order asked.

"No!" the man said. "Can't you get it right? I only wanted the fries to be a large."

"Could you try speaking more into the microphone?" the worker said. "I'm having a hard time understanding you."

"You're having a hard time understanding because you aren't listening," the man said. "Maybe you just need to get better equipment or have your hearing checked."

"What drinks did you want with the meals?" the worker asked.

"I told you I wanted a small Sprite and a large orange," the man said. "I really don't have time to be ordering everything twice."

There were a few more such exchanges. Elliana couldn't understand a lot of what the man said, so she assumed the worker, rather than receive any more of the man's wrath, was just putting in what he thought the man said. Finally, the worker told the man the price and asked him to pull forward to the serving window.

The worker who had taken the order turned to Elliana. "Did you hear all that? Wow! What a grouch."

After a couple of cars had pulled to the serving window, the offending customer pulled up. The girl at the window repeated what the order showed to make sure it was right.

The man really blew up. "Oh, for heaven's sake! Can't you

guys do your job? That hardly resembles what I ordered at all. The man then repeated the order so fast that the girl struggled to get the changes made. Twice more when she repeated it back, only to receive a rebuke. But finally, she had it right. By that time, she was almost in tears.

She moved from the window, and Elliana, as the girl's trainer, took over and had the opportunity to tell the guy that the fries were still cooking. She asked him to park in one of the waiting spots. Again, the man unleashed a verbal onslaught. By the time the man pulled around to park, half the workers were ready to tell him he could just go somewhere else to eat.

When the fries were ready, and the order was finished, everyone looked at each other to see if anyone would volunteer to deliver it. Finally, the guy who had first taken the order said he would.

"I'm just in the mood to give him a piece of my mind anyway," the worker said.

Many employees watched out the window as the meal was delivered. But instead of seeing a scene indicating there was a problem, there seemed to be a pleasant exchange. And when the worker turned to come back in, he was wearing a big grin. Everyone gathered around.

"What happened?" someone asked. "Did you tell him off?"

The worker shook his head. "I didn't have to. When I went to hand him his food, he said he needed to apologize. That really shocked me, so I didn't say anything. And then the man went on to say he needed to apologize because his daughter said he was mean."

The worker laughed and then continued. "I thought I would see maybe a teenager or someone older in the car, but when I looked in the back seat, there was a little girl in a car seat who was about three years old."

As everyone laughed, Elliana thought it was interesting to consider that a three-year-old could do what none of them could.

A Careful Job

My cousin, Becky, had her daughter and son-in-law moving up here to go to college. We invited them to come out to dinner when they finished. But as luck would have it, the truck loading took longer than expected, so it would be hours after the planned dinner time before they would arrive.

When Becky finally called, she said they were still a half-hour from their destination. She was going to take them some food because they wouldn't make it out for dinner. I said I would be happy to drive in and help unload the truck, and Becky's daughter gratefully accepted my offer.

The drive to town typically takes me about twenty minutes. But the temperature had dropped, freezing everything. The roads were slick, and at one point, a car was flipped on its top over an embankment. The police were already there, and traffic was moving slowly around the accident site.

Even though I thought I would beat the moving truck to the apartment, people were already unloading the truck when I arrived. I jumped in and helped, but it was slow going. The parking lot was like a skating rink, and everyone had to shuffle like penguins to keep from falling down. This was especially hard carrying boxes, mattresses, and couches.

The stairs up to the apartment were wobbly and instilled little confidence in their ability to hold a person's weight, especially when carrying something heavy. But everyone worked steadily and carefully, and it wasn't too long before the truck was unloaded.

But the moving truck couldn't hold everything, so they had loaded the more fragile items into cars. So, with even more care, we started unloading them. Often, even with something that was not too heavy, two people would each take an end. This offered stability walking across the ice, and if one of the two slipped, the other could hold tightly to the item so it wouldn't fall.

It was with just such a box of valuable pictures and nick-nacks that another of the men and I carefully made our way across the ice. It was slow going, and with a couple of almost falls, the box holding the items split open on one side, making getting the contents safely inside even more difficult. But with great care, we made it across the ice. Then, with the same slow process, we made it up the stairs and into the apartment. It was with great relief that we set the box down.

When we returned to the car, Becky's husband, Scott, had a basket full of fragile porcelain figurines. It was full and heavy, but he is strong and had a good grip on it. The basket was an awkward shape and was probably easier for him to carry alone. Otherwise, any of us would have offered to help. He slowly, cautiously made his way across the ice, and I breathed a sigh of relief when he made it to the stairs.

But Scott still had to carry the basket up to the apartment. With the stairs wobbling under his weight, he worked his way up each step. Once he reached the top, he was pretty much home free, and he soon had the basket inside. He had done a superb job, and I'm sure he felt proud of what he had done.

While Scott returned for another load, Becky was rummaging around in the car, apparently looking for something. When Scott finally made it back to the car, Becky pulled her head out and turned to him.

"Scott, did you take that basket full of porcelain items into the apartment?"

Scott smiled and nodded. "I sure did."

"Well," Becky said, "could you go get them? They were supposed to stay in the car."

And that reminded me of how, too often, when I feel I've done a good job, I instead find out I have done it all wrong.

Guaranteeing a Second Date

I always love hearing how married couples met. Recently, some neighbors shared their story.

Kaylie and Trent were both with their families at the same football game. However, even though they had family members who were friends, they had never met. The groups they were each with were sitting near each other, and the family members who were acquainted said hello.

As the game progressed, one of Kaylie's family members said, "You know, Kaylie, we really ought to set you up with Trent."

Meanwhile, one of Trent's family members suggested he ask Kaylie on a date. Trent was rather shy and wasn't about to ask someone he didn't know. So, the two families worked it out to introduce Trent and Kaylie to each other. And when they did, they openly suggested to Trent and Kaylie that they go on a date.

Trent realized it would be awkward not to ask her, so he did. They set up to go hiking, something they found they both enjoyed.

When the appointed day came, Trent picked Kaylie up, driving his nice, new truck. Kaylie thought Trent was good-looking, and she immediately liked his truck, too. She found out he used it in the rugged work he did, and she liked that as well.

Trent, on the other hand, wasn't sure about Kaylie. She was pretty, and she was nice. But she had more confidence in herself than he had ever dreamed of having. He had never seen that in a girl before. He liked that, and admired it in her, but at the same time, he wasn't sure he felt up to dating such a girl.

The plan was to walk a few miles through woods, then cross some sagebrush-covered hillsides to a shady meadow. They would have lunch there before returning. Trent had hiked with other girls and had to carry most of the lunch and water. But Kaylie took her share, and maybe more, and he admired her for that, too.

As they walked, they talked and enjoyed the scenery. It was a beautiful day, and the hike wasn't too strenuous. Everything was going well until the path turned along the sagebrush-covered hillside. Suddenly, a rattlesnake slithered out of the brush, blocked their path, and dared them to come any closer.

Unknown to Trent, Kaylie had worked on a ranch one summer that had lots of rattlesnakes. She had defended livestock and other farm animals from snakes many times.

Without even thinking, her defensive instinct kicked in, and she yelled, "Grab a stick!"

She grabbed one and drove the snake from the trail, with it seemingly feeling lucky to get away from her. When she turned to look for Trent, he was nowhere to be found.

He said do us, "I will admit, I ran screaming like a little girl all the way back to the truck. But in my defense, I had a bad run-in with a snake once, and I am deathly afraid of them."

When Kaylie got back to the truck and found Trent there, still breathing hard from the encounter on the trail, she knew the date was over. They didn't attempt to hike the trail again, nor did they even eat the lunch they had brought.

But during the time on the hike, while they had visited, Kaylie realized that Trent was a great guy, even if he was afraid of snakes. She knew that if she didn't do something before he dropped her off, that would be the last time she would see him. So when they pulled up to her house, and he got out to come around and open her door, she put her sweater in the back seat of his pickup on top of his tools. She knew he would see it when he went to work.

After walking her to her door, Trent felt bad. He really liked Kaylie, but how could he face her again after what had happened? He was embarrassed and, as he put it, "his manly pride was wounded."

But a couple of days later, he found her sweater, and he knew he should return it. So, he called her and told her about the sweater. "I can drop it off to you tonight after work."

"Don't make a special trip," she said. "Just bring it next time we go on a date."

That was just enough to give Trent the confidence to ask her out again. And, as they say, the rest was history.

Talking

It had been a while since we had foster children. They took the last little boy from our home and returned him to his mother. He and his two sisters lost their lives in a fire there. The mother didn't seem to care, while our hearts ached. It was hard to take children again. But then, one evening, we got a call from the social worker.

"We have three children who desperately need a home," he said. "Could you take one of them?"

"What about the other two?" my wife, Donna, asked.

"We'll keep looking for homes for them," came the reply. "We can't expect you to take three when you already have eight of your own."

Donna said we would discuss it, and she hung up the phone. She came to me and explained the situation.

"If we take any," I said, "I want to take all three. I don't want them separated."

Donna smiled. "Good. I thought that is what you would say, and I felt the same way."

We had watched our little foster boy struggle not being with his two sisters. They were young and had been placed in homes before he came to us. We had helped him call them almost every night. And even though he was concerned about going back to live with his mother and her boyfriend, he was excited to be with his sisters again. The tragedy that followed, and how much he had missed his sisters, steeled our resolve that if we could do anything about it, we would try to keep siblings together.

Donna called the social worker, and he was overjoyed. "But are you sure you want all of them?"

She assured him we would be happy to have all three. When he told us he would bring them over the next morning, we knew we had a long night ahead of us. I retrieved bunk beds from storage and set them up. Donna got bedding ready. The boys would share a room, and the girl would be in a room with one of our daughters.

When the social worker brought the children, they were immediately taken in by our children. They were off to show them around the yards, meet our animals, and get some food from the garden. Meanwhile, the social worker sat down to discuss challenges.

"Talia is almost four," he said. "But due to neglect, she has problems speaking. We will need you to take her to a speech therapist twice each week. We thought maybe she should have a couple of weeks to settle in, and then we will set the first appointment."

Since I would be at work, that fell to Donna, so they worked out the details. Within the first week, the children had settled into our family routine with chores, homework, and the meal schedule. There were challenges, as there always are when trying to integrate people from different backgrounds. But the one thing the children seemed to enjoy was mealtimes.

They had been used to finding whatever food they could on their own. Donna prepared excellent meals, and we always insisted on eating dinner together. It was a time for everyone to share about their day. The boys joined in right away. Talia was a little quieter, but within a few days she would express her thoughts and feelings, too, sometimes even telling us imaginative stories.

Eventually, Donna took Talia to her first speech session. When I came home, I asked, "So what do they say is wrong with her speech?" She had a bit of a lisp, but not more than most children.

Donna shrugged. "The speech therapist seemed confused at the report from Social Services and was going to check on it some more."

Donna took Talia to a couple more sessions, and the speech therapist said he was sending the social worker to visit with us. When the social worker arrived, he asked to see Talia. When she came, he asked her how she liked it with us. She told him about her new bed, about her new dolls, and lots of things. When she finished, he smiled and sent her back to play. He then said we didn't need to take her to speech therapy anymore.

"So what was her speech therapy supposed to fix?" I asked.

"She had never said a full sentence before she came here," he replied.

We were stunned. She talked as much or more than any of the children. When the social worker asked what we had done, we didn't know what to say.

"We just talked to her," Donna said, "and she responded."

The social worker nodded. "I guess that sometimes all a person needs is to have someone to talk to."

Upside-Down Plate Day

It was a crazy year. We had eight children of our own and had taken in three foster children. We also had two little girls who lived down the road come over for breakfast every morning. How that started was interesting, too. One freezing cold morning at the beginning of the school year, we saw Cindy and Lilly walking down to the corner to meet the bus. We invited them to come in and get warm and told them I would take them in the van with all the others. They were shivering and happily joined us.

Each day, our usual routine was for me to get up and start cooking pancakes and eggs as fast as I could. Soon all the children flooded into the kitchen. While I was getting everyone fed, Donna, my wife, was busy brushing hair, signing papers, and preparing everything the children needed for school. On the first morning, Cindy and Lilly came, Donna asked them if they had eaten breakfast. Cindy pulled a small bag of chocolate chips from her pocket that the two girls planned to share on the bus.

Donna shook her head. "That will never keep you until lunch. Go grab a plate."

I mixed up some more pancake mix, and soon the two little girls were heartily eating their way through the pile of pancakes covered in syrup. Our routine changed a little after that. The first thing I did each morning was to unlock the door before I started breakfast. Cindy and Lilly knew to come right in when they arrived, and they learned to do just like the other children. They went directly to the plate cupboard and got themselves a plate and utensils.

Cindy and Lilly also often joined the line each morning to have their hair brushed and put into piggy tails. We were most of the way through the school year when we learned something else about them. Their father worked nights, and while he did, their mother spent the night with other men. The girls were often home alone. That only came out in the divorce after their mother ran off with some man. Cindy and Lilly's father was a good man and was determined to take care of his little family. We took care of the girls even more, and often their little brother, too.

Though we were usually on time for the bus, sometimes with a busy morning, it was waiting for us when we pulled up. On one such morning, we were almost ten minutes late. I thought I would have to drive the children all the way to school. But the bus was still waiting. As the children piled out of the van and climbed aboard, I went over to visit with the bus driver.

"Thanks for waiting," I said.

She laughed. "Of course I'd wait. You bring almost half of my busload in your van."

We loved all the children, and over the course of the year, we all became like one big family. Cindy and Lilly's father even gave permission at the school for me to pick up his girls or take care of things there in his absence.

And then came Valentine's Day. My father-in-law had made it a tradition in his home to do something special for his family, and I carried on his tradition. I had to plan ahead and get up early, but when the children came into the kitchen for breakfast, the table was set, but every plate was turned over with candy stuffed under it.

Our oldest foster son, Kevin, came in and stared. "What in the world?"

My ten-year-old son, Scott, who came in behind him, said, "It's upside-down plate day."

Cindy and Lilly had joined them, and Cindy asked, "What's upside-down plate day?"

Scott smiled and went to his plate and turned it over. "That's the day Daddy stuffs candy under everyone's plates."

"It's also known as Valentine's Day," I said. "And no one gets any candy until after they have eaten a good breakfast."

They all hurried to eat so they could dig into their treats, but we made them save most of it for after school so they wouldn't be too hyper for their teachers. As we were heading out to the van, Cindy, Lilly, and some of the younger foster children gave me a hug.

"We've never had an upside-down plate day before," Lilly said.

"Us neither," Kevin added.

"Well, happy Valentine's," I replied. "And may you always remember that there are people who love you."

True Love

Eight-year-old Jason, one of our foster children, slammed his pencil down. "If you truly loved me, you wouldn't make me do things I hate, like this math!"

Jason had come to our home with his sister and brother. The three children were taken from their home because their mother needed medical help to stabilize her mentally, and their father played video games all day and didn't take care of them. The children had been left on their own to get food, get on the bus, and fend for themselves.

The boys often missed school, and when they did go, they showed the lack of care they were receiving. Though almost four, Talia had been left in a crib all day, often going hungry and having no interaction with anyone when her brothers weren't home.

Shortly after the children came to our home, we started receiving calls and letters from the boys' teachers. They were struggling with homework and other related items. Jason was especially having a hard time. He was held back in the same grade he was in the previous year but was still failing every subject.

Sitting in his chair at our kitchen table where I had been working with him, Jason glared at me. He was defiantly daring me to teach him.

"Jason," I calmly said, "love is not letting a person throw their life away when you know they have great potential. True love is helping them become the best they can be."

Jason's expression turned from one of anger to one of confusion. "What?"

"Jason, you can do this math. I know you can. You're a smart little boy. You have the ability to be the top student in your class. And I'm not willing to let you do or be less than you can be. However, that only comes through hard work."

Jason stared at me for a long time. Finally, he said, "When you make me work on the homework that I hate, it's because you love me?"

I nodded. "I want to see you become the best you can be, and I know you can do great things."

He just stared at me for a minute or so. It was evident that he had never thought of it that way before. Finally, he quietly opened his book, and we went back to work. It took a while to get the whole assignment right because I wouldn't just give him the answers. I made him work them and then showed him what he was not understanding. But a couple of days later, when he brought home a paper with a perfect score, it was the first time he didn't get a zero, and he was thrilled.

I wish I could say it was perfect after that, but it wasn't. Still, one success led to another. As he felt the joy of accomplishment, he sought more. My wife and I spent hours working with him on reading, writing, math, and all of his subjects. Soon he was bringing home high scores on every assignment.

After a few months, Jason brought home his grade report. He had nearly perfect grades in every subject. He also brought a letter from his teacher. She said he was the top student in her class in almost every area. He was now working hard and wasn't belligerent. She said Jason had top scores in nearly every attitude category, which pleased her even more than his grades. She ended with, "I don't know what you're doing, but keep it up."

When I read his grades, I praised him, and he just beamed. He smiled and said, "Love is helping someone do their best, and doing my best feels good."

As he ran off to join the other children, I thought that with all he had learned, his new understanding of what love truly is was probably the most important thing of all.

Heartbreaking Rules

One of the biggest challenges of being a foster parent is that those making the rules rarely understand those rules' heartbreaking effects. I realize lawmakers and judges have the best interest of the children in mind. Still, often a one-size-fits-all regulation does not work to the benefit of the children. That is the effect a rule change had on us.

The three foster children we had were thriving in our care. The two boys' grades had improved dramatically, and it looked like they would finish the school year near the top of their classes. Four-year-old Talia was now talking and was even learning her numbers and the alphabet. That is why, when the social worker called asking to come to visit, we had no concerns that there might be a problem.

When he came, we called the three children. They were happy and told him how much they loved being in our home. They then ran off to play. The social worker then turned to us and took a deep breath before talking.

"I want you to know that we are really pleased with how well the children are doing in your home. That is why it is so hard to tell you what I have to tell you."

My wife, Donna, and I looked at each other. Until that point, we had thought it was just a routine welfare check. The social worker didn't speak for a brief time, nor did he look at us, but finally, he looked up and began to talk.

"The state has changed the rules about how many children a family can have and still have foster children," he said. "I'm afraid we have to move the children from your home."

I felt like the air had been knocked out of me, and I could see tears in Donna's eyes. "But can't you tell them the children are doing well?" Donna said. "Can't you tell those in charge that?"

"We've tried to," the social worker said. "But they told us there are no exceptions. They feel if a family has too many children, they can't take care of more."

"But we all work together," I replied. "Our children help and love each other just as we love and work with them."

"I know," he replied. "I'm sorry. I did everything I could to let you keep the children."

"When will you take them?" Donna asked.

"Tomorrow," he replied.

He then asked if we wanted him to tell the children, but we declined, feeling it would be better if we did.

After he left, we called all the children together. It took some time to get our emotions under control so we could speak, and the children realized the gravity of what we had to say. When we finally were able to tell them, there were many emotions, both from our foster children and our own children. One of our foster sons ran to his room and slammed the door. Some of the children were angry. Most of them were crying.

The next day, when the social worker came, it was hard to say goodbye to the children. I don't care how many times we have had to do it, it has never gotten easier. But the social worker told us something that helped. He said the children's aunt, their mother's sister, was getting the children's mother some medical help and had applied to take the children.

The children ended up being in two homes during the last two weeks of school. They were angry, and the families struggled with them. But eventually, their aunt did get them and got their mother the medical help she needed. About six months after the children left our home, the aunt called and asked if they could come to visit.

We watched for them, and the minute they pulled up, our children rushed out to greet them with us close behind. The children's mother was doing better, and their home life was more stable. When they all came into our home, the aunt said, "The children wanted to bring us here."

Our oldest foster son said, "We just wanted them to feel the love we felt here."

As the children then ran off to play, I thought hearing that made all the heartache worth it.

Singing Bass

My wife is a music major, and most of our children have taken after her. Their extracurricular activities have been in band, choir, and theatre, so I have spent many hours attending concerts. One concert was quite memorable.

It had been a cold winter. Attendance had dropped at school because of illness, with talk of a short shutdown for everyone to get well. Colds were most common, and the flu wasn't far behind.

At this time, our daughter came home and informed us that she and three other girls had formed a Sweet Adeline group. They were going to be performing at a barbershop concert. Not only would it be fun, but they got extra credit for doing it.

The girls started practicing after school and on weekends because the concert was only a couple of weeks away. They were doing well until one of the girls got a nasty cold. It wasn't long before all four of them had it.

They debated pulling out of the concert. But the performance was only a day away, they had worked so hard, and some of the girls desperately needed the extra credit. They only had to sing one song, and they felt they could keep their distance from the other performers, perform their music, and leave.

But which song should they perform? They had practiced quite a few, but none of them sounded right. With their colds, the girls no longer ranged from near tenor to soprano, but were more like baritone to high tenor. They tried a few songs and then ended up settling on one that was more in a medium men's range. They felt awkward doing that, but they had to admit to themselves that it was what they needed to do.

The night of the concert came, and I could imagine our daughter, along with the rest of her group, nervously waiting backstage, feeling trepidation about singing a song meant for men. But as the announcer stepped to the microphone and started to speak, I had to smile. I had sung with him in a choir and knew he had a beautiful tenor voice. But as he spoke, his voice was a rough but solid bass. He announced the songs the men's group would sing and then stepped back to join the other twenty-three group members.

The men's group was the sponsor for this barbershop festival, and I had heard them sing many times. They had a nice, even balance between the bass, baritone, second tenor, and first tenor sections. But that was not the case this time. There was an overwhelming bass section. Apparently, they had the same problem as our daughter's group and had to have some of their members sing lower than usual.

As the concert progressed, almost every group had a similar problem. When our daughter's group sang their deeper-than-usual song, they fit in with everyone else. But the humorous clincher was the song the men's choir chose as their final number. They announced it was going to differ from what was listed in the program. Then they sang Mr. Bass Man. And when they ended, even the highest tenors hit the low notes on the ending.

"Oh, Mr. Bass Man, now I'm a bass man too. Ba-ba-ba-bah."

And the audience broke into thunderous applause for everyone who came and sang, even if they had to sing a little lower than usual.

Updating Everything

My wife, Donna, and I are hoping to build a new home. We realize that as we get older, our house, with its myriad of stairs, will not be sufficient for us. We have purchased some land and have started the impossible task of getting building permits, moving our current house contents into storage, and the millions of other jobs associated with building and selling.

As we wait for engineering and permits, we have started the arduous task of getting our home ready to sell. This has required multiple trips to the hardware store as we plaster, paint, and fix up anything that might be amiss in our home. On one of these trips, I ran into Barbara, a good friend I hadn't seen for a long time.

I have known Barbara and her husband for many years. Her husband passed away some time ago. Barbara had been a homemaker and had probably always felt her husband would be there to provide for their family. But his death left her with the challenge of making a living and dealing with many decisions in life. I had to admit that it surprised me to see her at the hardware store. The items a person would purchase there didn't seem like something that would interest her.

"So, what brings you here?" I asked.

"I'm replacing some cupboards, and I needed some knobs for the new ones," she replied.

That sounded reasonable for her. A new knob was one thing; a major repair was another.

"How about you?" she asked.

"I just replaced and patched some drywall, and the trim on the wall was old and worn out," I replied, holding up a piece of wood. "I hope to get some new trim to match the old so the repaired section will match the rest of the wall. If I can't match it, I might have to replace all of it in that room. It seems fixing a house is a never-ending project, with one thing leading to another."

Barbara nodded. "I totally understand that. What got you started?"

"We're preparing our house to put it on the market," I replied.

"Sounds like where I was after my husband died," Barbara said. "I decided there were a lot of things wrong with my house. I decided to sell it and buy a new one. But in reviewing the sales opportunities with a real estate agent, he told me I could get a lot more money if I updated and fixed some things first. So, I set about doing that, then continued fixing more."

"Did you do the repairs yourself?" I asked.

She shrugged. "A lot of them. But if I couldn't figure out how to do it on my own with the help of YouTube, I hired someone. I just about remodeled the entire house. It took nearly a year before the real estate agent and I felt it was ready to sell."

I was amazed at her initiative. "So, these new knobs are for your new house?"

Barbara shook her head. "No. You may remember that a few years ago we purchased some apartment complexes as an investment. When I finished with all the work on my own house, I realized those apartments needed new makeovers. I am about halfway through that job, and these knobs are for one of the apartments."

By this point, I was almost speechless. Not only had she taken on redoing her own house, but she was also now renovating the apartments.

"Donna and I are hoping to build a new home, and we'd love to see yours," I said. "Where do you live?"

"Don't you remember where I live?" she replied. "You've been there a hundred times."

"But I thought you bought a new house," I said.

Barbara laughed. "Heck, no. After I got everything done on mine, I realized my house was what I was looking for in my new one, so I just kept it."

Losing Pens

My mother lives in an assisted living center and doesn't drive anymore. Since I, of all her children, live the closest, she calls me, and I take her to where she needs to go. Recently, she needed to go deposit some money at the bank.

While we were there, she had to sign a document. When she picked up the pen, it reminded her of something she had already discussed with me.

She turned to me and said, "We still haven't gotten me any pens."

When I helped her set up the television in her apartment, I wanted to write instructions for her to find her way through the different channels she likes. The only pen we found in her apartment didn't write, so I used the marker I had purchased for her to mark her clothes. I had written on the back of the channel information guide she received from the assisted living center, but it bled through. That messed up the channel listing. This caused great consternation on her part, and I had promised to get her a new guide and some pens.

The lady at the bank said, "Why don't you take a couple of our pens? We have lots. We give out complimentary ones to our customers."

Mom was happy to oblige and took a few. As she put them into her purse, it reminded me of another time regarding pens at another bank.

I was a teenager, and my parents ran a farm implement business. For advertising, they ordered hundreds of pens with "Howard Equipment" emblazoned on the side of them. They weren't the fanciest pens, but they were pricey. Unique items like that were a lot more expensive than they are today.

To my parents' dismay, the pens started disappearing at an

alarming rate. A few came home in my father's pocket and were added to our collection there, but most seemed to walk out of the store with customers. I don't think they were intent on stealing them. I assume they either felt they were meant as gifts, or they inadvertently put them into their pockets after writing a check or signing a paper. Nonetheless, in almost no time at all, most of the pens were gone, and we were reduced to a frantic search to find something we could use to write.

My mother, who had gone to all the effort to buy the pens, was especially annoyed. She wanted to figure out a way to keep the pens around and always have them available. That was when she went to the bank and saw something for the first time that later became common. She saw a pen connected to a chain that was bolted to the counter.

She encountered it when she reached for something to fill out a deposit slip while she stood at the teller window.

Mom laughed as she held up the pen connected to the chain. "This is brilliant!"

The teller nodded. "We have had so many of our pens walk away that the manager paid someone to come in and chain them all down that way. It cost a lot to have it done, but we haven't lost a single pen since that day."

"I paid a lot of money for hundreds of pens with our Howard Equipment name on them," Mom said. "They have almost all disappeared."

"Isn't that just the most annoying thing?" the teller said. "Especially when you find them in other businesses around town."

Mom agreed and then went to sign her deposit slip. But as she did, she noticed the writing on the pen. It said, "Howard Equipment." When the teller realized what was there, it embarrassed her.

Mom got a complimentary bank pen that day, too.

All Day in the Saddle

(Part 1)

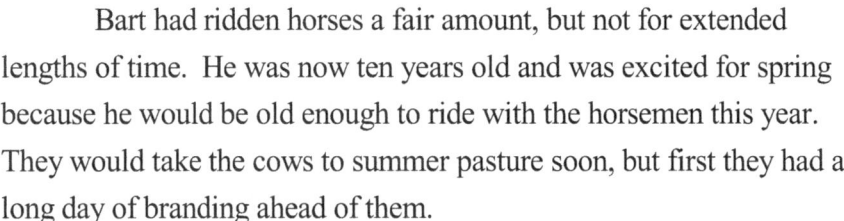

Bart had ridden horses a fair amount, but not for extended lengths of time. He was now ten years old and was excited for spring because he would be old enough to ride with the horsemen this year. They would take the cows to summer pasture soon, but first they had a long day of branding ahead of them.

Bart had begged his dad to let him be one of the riders who brought the cows into the corral. His dad had reminded him it would mean a full day in the saddle.

"Are you sure you're up to that?" his dad asked. "A person can get really sore when they're not used to it."

Bart assured his dad that he could handle it.

"All right," his father said. "But I don't want to hear any complaining if it turns out to be harder than you thought."

On branding day, the men were up before sunup, and Bart was the first one to the kitchen. He could hardly contain his excitement. It was all his mother could do to get him to eat.

"You are going to have a hard day, and you need a good breakfast," she said.

Bart hurriedly ate what she set before him, and then he was on his way to get his horse saddled. He would ride Red, an older roan-colored horse that Bart's father said knew more about cutting and moving cattle than most men. He wouldn't have to direct her much other than to show her which cows they wanted. Then his job was to just hold on. Bart had cut cows out of the herd a few times on Red. More than once, when she turned with the cow, he hadn't been holding on tight enough, and Red had left him in the dirt. But he was older and more experienced now, and he knew better.

Bart's older brother, Seth, rode up alongside him as they

headed to where the cows were.

"Are you sure you're up to an entire day of hard riding?" Seth teased.

Seth was only a couple of years older than Bart, and it always annoyed him that their father treated Seth like a grown man, while he was treated like a boy.

"Of course I am," Bart replied. "You'll see."

All the riders circled the cows and brought some to the branding corral. There were too many cows to do them all in one group. The men on horses then split up. Some worked in the corral to move cows to the branding chute. Others stayed outside to chase down any cow that got loose. As they moved the different groups of cows through, the horsemen traded who was on which assignment.

By the time the sun was approaching the horizon, and the last of the cows were moving through the chute, Bart was so tired he could hardly hold on when Red took off after a cow. But finally, the last cow returned to the pasture, and the horsemen rode off to take care of their horses. When Bart slid from Red's back and tried to take a step, he nearly collapsed. His legs felt like rubber, and his backside hurt worse than anything he could remember.

Seth laughed at Bart's predicament. "Didn't I warn you? But there is something that will help your saddle blisters—turpentine."

"Turpentine?" Bart replied.

Seth nodded. "You remember how Mom rubs it on you when you have sore muscles? It's just the thing. It will make you forget all about your hard day of riding."

Bart could remember how good turpentine felt on his sore muscles. So, as soon as he arrived at the house, he got the turpentine bottle and retired to the bathroom. He got a giant cotton ball and soaked it in turpentine. He swiped it across his backside. Instantly, a scream he could not contain came from his throat.

Bart could hear Seth's laugh even above his mother's

concerned voice asking if he was all right. Panting to smother the pain, Bart said he was okay. When he emerged from the bathroom, Seth was waiting for him.

"Wasn't I right? Didn't the turpentine on your blisters make you forget about the hard day of riding?"

"Yes," Bart replied. "Now, all I can think of is revenge or murder."

Sweet Revenge

When Bart's brother, Seth, tricked him into putting turpentine on his saddle sores, Bart was determined he would get revenge. Bart was ten, and Seth, being a couple of years older, often played pranks on him. Bart wanted the revenge to cause Seth to think twice about ever tricking him again.

Bart thought all day about what he could do. He was still deep in thought about it as he finished up chores for the evening, feeding the family rabbits and cleaning their pens. At dinner that evening, he was so quiet that his mother asked him if he was okay.

Bart nodded. "I have just been thinking about some things."

"Anything we can help with?" she asked.

Bart shook his head. "No. Just thinking."

She then turned to Seth. "Seth, it's your birthday this Saturday. Is there any special cake you would like?"

Seth grinned. "Chocolate. The more chocolate, the better."

After dinner, everyone helped clean up, and then most of the family went to watch television. Bart decided to get a piece of the chocolate bunny he had received for Easter a few days earlier. He broke off an ear and was just about to bite into it when he had a brilliant idea.

While everyone was busy, Bart went to the kitchen and retrieved a pan, a spoon, and a hot plate burner their family sometimes used at hotels when they traveled. Clutching his chocolate bunny tightly in one hand with the kitchen items in the other, he made his way to the barn. Remembering how his mother made chocolate-dipped pretzels at Christmas, he turned the burner on low and put a large piece of his chocolate bunny in the pan. Then, while the chocolate melted, he went and got a couple of handfuls of the biggest, hardest bunny poops he could find.

When the chocolate was ready, he expertly dipped the bunny poops into the chocolate. He would let them cool, then redip them until they were the size of the malt balls that he got in his Easter basket. When they were done, he let them cool. He did plenty, and when he finished, he chose the best ones and destroyed the others. He then cleaned up the mess and returned the kitchen items.

Bart could hardly wait for Saturday. When it finally came, he asked his mother if he could help decorate Seth's cake. "I've saved some of my Easter candy specially for Seth's piece of the cake," he said.

His mother smiled and nodded. "That's really sweet that you want to do that for your brother."

Bart's mother decorated most of the cake, but on one part, Bart made the number 13 using his newly created bunny malts. The cake was beautiful.

After dinner, when it came time for the cake, they all sang to Seth. Once he blew out the candles, Bart requested he get to cut the cake.

"That's only fair," their mother said. "You helped decorate it."

Bart cut the entire section with the 13 for Seth's piece. He cut other pieces for everyone else. As they all dug in, Bart could hardly contain his smile when he saw Seth's eyes widen as he took his first bite, one with a giant bunny malt on it.

In a loud voice, Seth said, "This cake tastes like. . ."

Seth paused and looked at his father. Bart knew that one thing their father didn't allow was any criticism of the food their mother made. That could bring a heavy punishment.

"Is there a problem, son?" their father said tersely. Seth shook his head. "Then I suggest you finish your cake."

Seth ate it, grimacing as he did. But later, when he and Bart were alone, he asked Bart if his cake tasted funny.

"Not mine," Bart said. "But did you know that bunny poop dipped in chocolate makes perfect-looking malt balls?"

"You are so dead!" Seth yelled, realizing what he had eaten.

"Maybe you can wash the taste out of your mouth with a little turpentine," Bart teased. "After all, it works on saddle sores."

Things We Have Lost

I ran the item over the scanner. "Peanut butter—four-thirty."

After the machine read the checkout amount, I paused. We have lost so many things over this last year, and this felt like a symbol of much of it.

I thought about when I was a boy, and the first time I could remember going with my mom to the grocery store. I was only about three, and I walked along, holding onto the edge of the shopping cart. I felt I was too big to ride in it. Besides, I had a new baby brother who claimed that space.

I felt amazed at the size of the store. It was the biggest building I had ever been in. That store today would fit in the checkout area of a typical department store, but back then, it was the biggest commercial building in town besides the theater. As we shopped, I felt a small child's wonderment seeing three brands of soap, four kinds of cereal, and two types of peanut butter. I thought it had to be the most amazing store in the world.

When we got in the checkout line, the lady ahead of us turned around. She greeted my mother by name and asked about our family.

"Well, if you can believe it," my mother replied, "our oldest son is now in high school."

"Wow!" the lady said. "Time really flies. I remember when you and your husband had just gotten married. How many children do you have, now?"

My mom pointed at my baby brother, who was cooing and trying to stick his whole fist into his mouth. "This is our ninth."

"Oh, my goodness," the lady said, patting my little brother like he was a lump of bread dough, "aren't you the cute little one."

My mother and the lady talked until it was the lady's turn to checkout. When it was our turn, the checker also greeted my mother by name. My mother smiled. "Bob, you aren't usually up here at the checkout stand."

Bob nodded. "True. But Anita is in the hospital having a baby."

They visited the whole time Bob punched each item's price into the machine and then put it into a paper bag. After Mom finished paying, Bob handed her a sucker. "This is for your little helper," he said, smiling at me.

Growing up in that small town, I knew every checker, and they knew me. At one point, Jason, one of the young men that bagged groceries, got sick. Jars were put on the checkout stands, and everyone put in their spare change. Jason was a cheerful, positive young man, and everyone loved him. The jars filled up repeatedly.

After lots of operations and many prayers, Jason started to recover. Everyone was relieved when he returned, even though he was thin and still weak from his ordeal. And Jason decided it was his turn to give back to those who had supported him. He made lots of personal notes with kind thoughts and slipped them into the customers' bags at the checkout. He did that until he could no longer work, and the original health problem took him from us.

Over the years, the communities I have lived in have gotten bigger, and so have the stores I have shopped at. Even so, when I have checked out, I have tried to connect with the checker, the person behind me in line, or the person ahead. Maybe it's nothing more than a friendly word or a smile at a young child in the shopping cart.

But Covid has taken much of that. Many orders are now online. And when we do shop at a store, the masks have covered our smiles. Still, I have tried to make some semblance of kinship through muffled talk through a mask.

So, when one of the biggest local department stores went to mostly self-checkout, I felt I, and possibly others, have lost even more. Yes, it is faster, but going through life at high speed does not always yield the happiest results. The machine announcing the price of the item doesn't care how anyone feels, if their children are in high school, or if someone is sick.

I guess we will all have to try even harder to find different ways to connect with people in our community.

Getting Mail

As my mother has gotten older, she has lived with some of her children for a time. I was the last one she lived with before choosing to go into an assisted living center. "It's not that I don't like living here," she said. "You make me quite comfortable. It's just the stairs and the tub."

We knew those might be a problem. We had fixed a room for her that had a bathroom nearby, put in a television, and tried to think of anything she might need. But there were stairs to climb. She mostly only had to do it once in the morning and once in the evening, as she spent the rest of the day downstairs with us. But even those two times were hard on her, and she needed oxygen to do it.

We also didn't have a walk-in shower. We got a shower chair she could sit on and then swing her legs into the tub. That worked okay, but it wasn't her favorite way to bathe. We told her we could help her, but she said she would rather have a stranger's assistance. So, we suggested having a Home Health Services worker come a few days each week. That was when she contemplated the idea of going to an assisted-living center.

It was not a nursing home, but a place where they would only help with the things that the person requested. She wanted to visit one that was owned by a family she knew, so we set up an appointment, and my wife and I took her to look at it.

After our visit, she struggled with the decision, so we suggested she make a list of pros and cons. Mom loves to garden, and one of the biggest cons on the list was that she wouldn't be able to. The staff there assured her she could fill her windows with plants if she wanted. With that promise, and the fact that she found out a few of her friends were already there, she decided to try it.

While she was getting settled in, I was there every day. I made sure she had books from the library, furniture she needed from the store, and lots of plant boxes for her windows. She found even more friends there and began feeling more and more comfortable.

Not long after she started living there, her ninety-fifth birthday came. We held a big birthday dinner for her at our house featuring her favorite foods. Some of my children and nieces and nephews came. I picked Mom up early and, once at our home, I connected her to Zoom where family and friends from all over could visit with her. Meanwhile, my wife and I finished preparing the meal.

We all had a good time. But afterward, as she and I were heading back to the assisted living center, I sensed that she felt something was missing. I asked her if there was anything else she needed.

She thought a minute and then said, "Yes, there is. I seldom get mail anymore."

I joked that I would bring my bills to her so she could open them, but she didn't think that was funny.

"Seriously," she said, "even when I was getting bills, at least I felt like people knew I was alive."

I thought a lot about that as I helped her to her room. After she showed me how much her plants had grown, she held up one of my seed catalogs. "I hope you don't mind me taking this. You had a lot, so I didn't think you would miss it."

I told her she was welcome to it, so she took it to look through as she laid down to rest. As I drove home, I thought about her comment about not getting mail and wondered what I could do about it. Then I had this brilliant idea. When I got home, I looked up gardening sites and signed up for Mom to receive a catalog from every place that had one. Then, every time I'd visit, I'd look to see if she had received any.

Finally, the first one arrived. "Look what came in the mail," she said, happily holding up a seed catalog.

They seemed to come in a torrent after that. It seemed like every time I went to visit, she had a new one sitting on her table. She even ordered a few things, and I got her some more potting soil and planting boxes so she could grow what she bought.

Finally, I knew things were better when, one night, after receiving another new catalog, she said, "As long as the seed companies know I'm alive, life is still worth living."

Taking Responsibility

Mrs. Ward was known as a strict teacher, and we experienced it firsthand. Of course, her sternness might have been out of necessity. Our eighth-grade social studies class consisted of fifty-four rambunctious boys and was the last period of the day. As a group, we seemed to oscillate between overly energetic one day to half asleep the next.

Mrs. Ward's class rules stated that if she caught someone doing something wrong or causing trouble, they would be immediately sent to the principal for disciplinary measures. Capital punishment with a big wooden paddle was still considered appropriate in that era. If she set forth a punishment, no questions were asked, and the person was marched off to what we often joked was the torture chamber.

Her rules also said that if someone did something wrong, and she couldn't figure out who it was, then the class must tell her. If no one would, the entire class would be punished. Though we had been in class almost an entire year, we had never had a full class punishment. Nothing ever seemed to get by Mrs. Ward. She had an uncanny ability to always know who the perpetrator was, even when she was writing on the board and had her back to the class.

It was late May, and we were winding up our final studies about Europe, when that changed. Mrs. Ward had frequently traveled to Europe and loved that section of the class. Unfortunately for me, with it being May, I was ready to be out of school and working on the farm. It took every ounce of discipline I could muster to sit in that seat for an hour.

Mrs. Ward said we had worked hard that week, so on Friday she would show us some slides from her trips to Europe. She said we wouldn't have to have any homework for the weekend. That sounded good. But on that Friday, the slides seemed to go on forever. I felt like if I had to see one more cathedral, I was going to go crazy.

At that point, she showed us a church that was bombed in World War II and had been beautifully restored. My pent-up energy got the best of me and took over my mental reasoning. I started making airplane bomber noises. Mrs. Ward immediately flipped the lights on.

"Who was making those dreadful noises?" she demanded.

In my defense, I thought they were pretty good, accurate sounds. Still, I knew I was in big trouble. However, no one answered. Lenny mouthed to me, "No one will tell on you."

"Well then," Mrs. Ward said, "if no one wants to tell me who it was, you will all be punished. You each have a five-page paper on the destruction of European cathedrals during World War II due next week, and you can spend part of your lunch hours working on it."

The entire class groaned, but still no one showed any sign of ratting me out. I looked at all my friends, willing to take a punishment to protect me, and I knew I couldn't live with knowing I had let that happen.

I slowly raised my hand. "It was me, Mrs. Ward."

The look on her face changed from one of anger to one of shock. "You realize you will be severely punished?" she asked. I nodded, so she said, "Why would you admit it if no one would tell on you?"

"Because it's not fair for everyone to have a punishment that should be mine alone, and if a teacher punishes students, the punishment should at least be fair."

I didn't mean it as a criticism of her class rules. I was just stating how I felt. I hadn't realized how it had sounded until Lenny drew his hand across his throat as if to say, "You're dead!"

The expression on Mrs. Ward's face was hard to judge. She paused briefly, then said, "Daris, you will stay after class." She then turned off the lights and continued the presentation.

When class ended, and everyone had gathered their books to leave, Lenny said, "I'll put some flowers on your grave."

After everyone was gone, Mrs. Ward said, "I've never had anyone admit it was them when I didn't know. And your expression of justice has made me reconsider my methods."

Instead of sending me to the principal, I had to do the extra papers, but I always felt good that I took the blame that was mine.

A Dream for a Salesman

Celese sighed as she climbed out of bed. She knew it was going to be a long day. She had some critical deadlines for work, and it always seemed like there was more to do than she could get done.

She took a quick shower and then made breakfast for her family. She fed everyone and got her husband off to work. Her young children sat down to watch Sesame Street, and Celese figured she had at least a half-hour to get some reports done before they were due at ten. But as she moved to the desk and pulled out her computer, Annalee, her four-year-old daughter, came and stood beside her.

"Mommy, do you want to hear about my dream last night?" she asked.

Always the good mother, Celese put her work aside. "Sure, honey. Tell me about it."

"Well," Annalee said, "there was this pony. And he was my friend. And he wanted me to go with him on a long trip."

As Annalee continued, Celese could feel her blood pressure increase. She wanted to listen to her daughter, but her mind was caught up with her concern about the approaching deadline. She could see the big clock in the living room from her vantage point, and it seemed to be moving at an increasingly faster rate.

Then the phone rang. Celese answered it. After talking for a minute, she briefly excused herself from Annalee's storytelling and retrieved some information for the friend who called. Annalee followed her, and as Celese returned to her desk, Annalee leaned against her and picked up the story of her dream from where she left off.

"And there was a pretty rainbow that had a doll sitting below it. . ."

The phone rang a few more times, and Celese would deal with the call, then return to listen to Annalee's story. Celese knew she wasn't doing well at anything. Though she was trying to focus attention on her daughter, her mind was deep in thought about her work.

Then the phone rang again. Celese thought to herself that the phone hardly rang on a typical day. But when she was busiest with the most critical issues, it was seldom quiet.

Celese picked up the phone. "Hello," a man said. "Did you know the warranty on your car is about to expire? I can extend it for you."

Celese tried unsuccessfully a couple of times to tell the man that she was not interested in a new warranty for her car, but he kept talking over her. Finally, in exasperation, she handed the phone to her little daughter.

"Annalee, why don't you tell this man about your dream?"

Annalee excitedly took the phone. She was seldom given a chance to talk on it unless a relative called.

"So," Annalee said into the phone, "there was this pony. And he was my friend. And he wanted me to go with him on a long trip."

The man tried to talk over Annalee, but she ignored him and continued with her dream. Celese went back to work. After a while, she could hear the dial tone on the phone Annalee was holding, but Annalee continued talking about her dream.

Eventually, Annalee said, "Okay, that's it," and handed the phone back to her mother.

That evening, after Annalee had a bath and curled up in Celese's lap, Celese said, "Annalee, you never finished telling me the rest of your dream."

"Oh," Annalee said sleepily. She then told a much more condensed version than she told the salesman, falling asleep as she ended.

Celese sat and rocked her sleeping daughter for a while, then tucked her into bed to let her have another sweet, four-year-old dream.

Worth It

Grant and Emma had just seen the last of their children married. Grant was almost sixty, and Emma was only a couple of years younger. They now talked about all the wonderful things they would do together during their retirement years. Then the Covid virus came.

It was only a couple of months after everything started shutting down when Emma came down with a cough. Grant was concerned, but Emma assured him it was probably nothing more than a cold. But as her cough and complications became worse, Grant pressed her to go to the hospital. She resisted as long as possible, but eventually her condition worsened until she relented.

Grant got Emma to the hospital, and shortly after they arrived, she slipped into a coma. He wanted to be with her, but the head nurse wouldn't let him.

"I'm afraid that Covid restrictions don't allow anyone in except hospital workers."

Grant fell into a chair in the waiting room. He didn't know what to do. Emma was his whole life. He wanted to be with her, to help her, to take care of her. Suddenly, the head nurse's words came back to him. He stood and walked to the hospital administrative office and asked to speak to the human resource director.

"May I help you?" the director asked.

"Am I right in assuming you're looking for additional help?" Grant asked.

"Yes," the director said. "We have been shorthanded since the Covid hit."

"I would like to apply to work here," Grant said.

"What nursing experience do you have?" the director asked.

"I have taken care of my wife and our six children when they've been sick."

The director looked at Grant skeptically, so Grant explained that his wife was in the hospital, and he wanted the job so he could be near her. "I'm a good worker," he added.

"You realize it doesn't pay well and could be dangerous?" the director asked. "You could get Covid and die."

Grant said he was aware of the risks. The director considered it briefly, then nodded. He had the secretary help Grant through the paperwork, and Grant started his new job the next evening.

Being a professor, Grant taught college classes on Zoom during the day and then worked the evening shift at the hospital. Soon he was well known for his diligent work ethic and his attentiveness to patients. One nurse said she felt their losses would have been higher without his help.

Each evening after his shift ended, he would sit by Emma's bedside and read to her as he held her hand. Sometimes he felt like there were small signs she knew he was there, a slight smile or the tiniest movement of her hand.

Months went by, and many patients came and went. But Emma's condition never changed. But then, after four months, it did. But not for the better. Her blood clots worsened, and she struggled to breathe, even with the help of machines.

Then the night came that she opened her eyes for just a brief moment and smiled at Grant as he read to her. He pulled her into his arms, and she spoke briefly to him, then she was gone.

Grant was the only family member at the funeral, though their children and grandchildren connected in with hundreds of others on Zoom. Grant spoke, sharing his love for Emma. But as he did, he struggled to control his cough.

Grant soon was in the hospital himself, struggling to breathe. For a couple of weeks, no one was sure he would live, but then he started to get better. When he had sufficiently healed, he came back to work to help all he could. One day, the human resources director stopped to visit with him.

"Grant, you've worked here for months, and I understand you only got to speak briefly to your wife. You struggled with Covid and nearly died. Has it all been worth it?"

Granted nodded. "That moment made it all worth it. As Emma was leaving, she told me she loved me. But then she said, 'I knew you were here for me. Now it's my turn to be there for you.'"

"But she's gone," the director said.

"Yes," Grant replied. "But sometimes I sense she is with me and always will be. Not even death can separate our love."

A Wild Ride

After reading my story about Sandy, a kitten we rescued, I received a letter from Steve Ciha. Steve reads my stories that appear in his newspaper and has written me a few times. He shared his own story about rescuing kittens.

A feral cat had decided to make her home on their property. They tried to befriend the cat, but it was too wild and would have nothing to do with them. One day, Steve's granddaughter came and told them the cat had three kittens in their flower bed. But having been discovered, the cat quickly moved her kittens.

Sometime later, the mother cat was found dead on the driveway. Steve found it strange that he or anyone else would have run over her. They all loved animals, and she should have been easy to see since there was nothing to hide behind. Steve wasn't sure how it could have happened without anyone knowing it.

With the mother cat dead, they knew the kittens would need help, and they put great effort into finding them. But it was to no avail. Finally, Steve had to leave for town, a seventy-mile round trip, so his effort in the search ended for the day. However, the following morning, as he was leaving, Steve saw something lying on the ground behind his truck. It was a tiny orange kitten, and it looked like it was dead. He picked it up and stroked it, and it feebly raised its head. Steve's wife, Vicki, immediately took charge of the situation. An eyedropper was found, milk was warmed, and the kitten was delicately fed. Slowly it gained strength. A cardboard box was located, and with a clean towel and a heating pad, the kitten did well. But where were the other two kittens?

The search was renewed. They searched the buildings and the woods for any place they thought a cat was likely to hide her kittens. But it was all for naught.

Steve had to make the trip to town again and left the others to the search, but he thought a lot about the kittens. How could the mother not have been seen and gotten run over? Why was the one kitten on the driveway behind his truck? Where could the other kittens be? When he got home, he found no one had had any luck in finding the other kittens. They knew time was running out if the kittens were to be saved.

Steve and Vicki went to take a walk in a nearby park, and as they returned home, Vicki said she could hear kittens. They zeroed in on the sound and realized it was coming from near the back of Steve's truck. Thinking about all the questions he had, Steve started putting the ideas together. The mother was run over unseen, and the kitten was on the ground behind his truck. Could the kittens be in the spare tire? Getting down on his hands and knees and peering underneath the truck, Steve could see little paws sticking through the spare tire lug nut holes.

Steve reached over the tire and lifted out the kittens one at a time. They had survived without their momma for three days and a hundred forty miles of travel. They were still alive, but just barely. However, with Vicki's attentive care, the kittens were soon mending.

Two of the kittens grew big and powerful, males for sure, and they were named Jack and Nala. At times everyone wondered if the small female would live, but she did, and they named her Clover for good luck. In time, they outgrew the cardboard box, the bathtub, and the bathroom, so they roamed the house and claimed it as their own.

Steve's granddaughter begged them to keep all three. A friend needed a cat, so they gave him Nala. But they decided they had to keep Clover and renamed her Baby.

They also decided to keep Jack, since he probably saved the others by finding his way out of the tire. They were

Jack, the cat

three beautiful kittens who had grown up to be wonderful cats.

If cats had a Mothers' Day, these kittens would make their mother proud.

A Date with Grandma

It's nice to be getting back to normal life again, even though that normal still feels strange. I am still teaching most of my classes online this semester, but I do have the privilege of teaching one computer science class face-to-face. We have had to social distance and wear masks, but the conversations I have enjoyed with my students before and after classes have returned.

One conversation that is always common is dating. Most of the time, when this conversation comes up, I simply listen. I usually come away grateful I do not have to go through those trying experiences anymore. During one such conversation, I listened as a girl named Cindy shared her experience from the previous night with Tina, one of her programming team members. Cindy worked as a waitress at a local restaurant and talked about a boy who had come in.

"He came with his grandmother," Cindy said. "He said it was her birthday, and he was taking her out for dinner."

"That's really sweet," Tina replied.

Cindy nodded. "I thought the same thing, and I told him so. But I especially thought that was the case when I learned how unpleasant she was."

"What do you mean?" Tina asked.

"She complained about everything," Cindy replied. "She complained about her aches and pains. She said she didn't eat out much when she was young, and young people today have so much money. She said the youth don't understand how hard things used to be. It continued like that during the entire meal."

"It's a wonder he took her out," Tina said.

"Every time she griped, he just quietly listened," Cindy said. "He never complained at all. And when he smiled at me, it just made me melt."

"Did you do anything to let him know you liked him?" Tina

asked.

Cindy nodded. "I definitely flirted with him, and he flirted back. I was sure he liked me, too. But the more we flirted with each other, the more it seemed to annoy his grandmother. So, I especially tried to make their meal perfect. Still, his grandmother said it was too tough to chew, even though he said it was very delicious. But that was also when he told me his name."

"That's a good start," Tina said.

"Yes," Cindy replied. "But when he went to tell me his last name, his grandmother stopped him. She said a person shouldn't give their name to strangers because they might use it against them. I thought I would never be able to connect with him. But then, when I gave them the bill, I saw him turn it over, take a pen, and write on it. I was sure he was writing his phone number or something."

Tina laughed. "You're lucky."

"But the night wasn't over, nor was his grandmother through," Cindy said. "I heard her telling him off for giving his phone number to someone he didn't know. And when I came back to get the payment, what he had written on the back of the receipt had been crossed out with lipstick."

"Oh, what bad luck," Tina said.

"I thought the same thing," Cindy replied. "But then I realized I was holding a receipt he had signed, as well as a credit card with his name on it. And to top it off, when I told the story to others in the kitchen, the cook said she had something that might remove the lipstick so we could see the number. I think it was lemon juice or something, and it worked."

"Awesome!" Tina said. "So, are you going to call him?"

Cindy grinned. "I already did. We have a date set for tomorrow night."

At that point, Tina high-fived Cindy.

Cindy laughed and said, "And we both agreed we won't tell his grandmother."

Flowers and Meaning

My mother, my brother, and I were making plans for Memorial Day. I would pick up my mother, and my brother's family and my family would meet at the cemetery that morning. When we had finished decorating the graves, we would go to my house for a barbecue.

"Can you bring lilacs with you?" my mother asked. "Lilacs are one of my favorite flowers."

My mom had just been to our house for Sunday dinner, and before she left, I cut her a bouquet of lilacs. She was still enjoying their fragrance.

"When I die," she said, "make sure you bring lilacs to put on my grave."

"I'm quite partial to mums, myself," my brother said. "Our lilacs are past blooming, so I think I will stop at the store and buy some mums to bring."

"What about you, Daris?" my mom asked. "What flowers do you like best?"

I thought about that question. Though I enjoy the fragrance and beauty of flowers, I must admit that what I like most is tied more to feelings and memories. I've grown roses, irises, tulips, and just about every type of flower. I love to watch my wife and children enjoy them. I also like to see the children carry them in to their mother. But strangely, the flower that brings the fondest memories is one I don't even grow, at least not on purpose. That flower is the dandelion.

I remember as a boy going into the pasture and seeing a sea of yellow and thinking it was the most beautiful sight in the world. But even more, I loved to see the wonder in the faces of my own children when the flower we too often think of as a noxious weed filled the countryside with a golden hue.

Only a couple of weeks ago, my two-year-old granddaughter was going across the yard, stopping to pick the small flowers. Each time her chubby little fist couldn't hold anymore, she would come and deposit them on my lap for safekeeping.

I thought of her own mother as a little girl. She would pick the dandelions. When I would get home from a long day of work, she would bring them to me in a cup of water her mother had helped her arrange.

"Here are some daddy wyons for you," she would say. "I picked them specially for you because you're my daddy."

I would pull her onto my lap and give her a big hug. Then I would often read a story to her, or we would sing a children's song together.

Over the years, almost all my children brought me bouquets of "Daddy lions." When they were small, they thought their daddy was the smartest and best guy in the world. But then they grew up, and as they did, daddy seemed less and less competent. When they became teenagers, to them daddy's esteemed value seemed to turn into an exponentially downward spiral until he was old-fashioned and knew next to nothing about what was good for them. That finally seemed to turn around some when they married and had children of their own.

Still, dandelions remind me of what I felt were some of the best times of my life. They remind me of working in the yard or playing in the park with my family. They remind me of picnics, hikes, and camping trips together. But mostly, they remind me of my love for them and pulling them onto my lap for a hug, a story, or a song.

When my granddaughter finished gathering dandelions and brought the last bunch to me, she gave a big handful to me and took the rest to give to her daddy. So, when my mom asked me what flowers I loved best, to her surprise, I had an unusual, but ready, reply.

"I just hope my children will bring me handfuls of Daddy Lions to put on my grave when I'm gone."

Getting Old

A sweet, elderly lady that goes to our church approached me after the Sunday meeting was over. Her son was helping her walk down the aisle. The son is almost seventy, so this mother was no spring chicken.

"I'm so sorry about missing your daughter's reception last night," the lady said to me. "That is one thing about getting old; I forget important things more and more all the time."

"The thing I hate about getting old," the son chimed in, "is the aches and pains. When I try to get some work done, I feel the effects of it for days."

The lady turned to her son. "Old, my foot! You don't know anything about getting old. I could still remember important things at your age, and though there were a few aches and pains, they were nothing like when you get to my age. When you get past eighty, the aches and pains are not a now-and-then thing caused by work. They are a constant caused by living."

"But at your age, you can slow down," the son said. "You don't have as many things you need to do."

"Or maybe it is just that there are more things I can't do," the mother said.

I laughed. "I heard a quote once that was attributed to Kathryn Hepburn. I don't know if she said it or not, but I really like it. It was claimed she said she dreaded getting old and not being able to do all the things she wanted. But she said when she got old, it was all okay because she didn't want to do anything anymore."

The sweet old lady turned and frowned at me. "Maybe she didn't want to because trying to do the slightest bit of work, or anything, makes you feel too miserable, and nothing seems to work right."

"What do you mean?" I asked.

"Your insides don't cooperate at all," she replied. "Either you're constipated so you're bound up all day, or you're running to the bathroom every ten minutes. And you have no muscle control, so you don't always make it when you do run."

"Mom, that's probably TMI," the son said.

She ignored him and continued. "And don't even get me started about my eyes. I have to have glasses to read. I have to have different ones to watch television. I need another pair that is for everyday use. I get the wrong ones on and miss half of what I'm watching on tv. Of course, that's okay when it is the news. Half of it isn't worth watching anyway, and the other half you wish you had never seen."

"Mom," the son said, "I'm sure Daris has other things to do."

She looked at him and glared. "Oh, and then there's driving. Or should I say, then your kids think you're too old to drive and take away the keys?"

"Mom," the son said, "you got in a wreck the last three times you tried to drive."

"Hitting the mailbox does not count as a wreck," she replied haughtily. "Besides, who was the idiot who put the mailbox so close to the driveway?"

"The mailbox has been in the same place for fifty years," the son replied. "Besides, the other times weren't mailboxes."

"What do you think insurance is for?" she replied.

The son sighed. "Mom, you're way off the topic you wanted to talk to Daris about."

She looked surprised. "I wanted to talk to Daris about something?"

The son nodded. "Remember? You wanted to talk to him about missing his daughter's wedding reception."

"Oh, yes," she said, turning back to me. "I wanted to apologize for missing your daughter's wedding reception last night."

"It's okay," I replied. "And it was actually not last night. It was the week before."

She looked shocked. "Now I know I am getting old. I realize it wasn't the reception I forgot last night."

"What was it?" I asked.

"It was Lawrence Welk," she replied. "And if I miss that, I feel I might as well be dead."

Perspective

Trevor came in late, as usual, into my linear algebra class. We were about four weeks into the semester, and he always missed at least the first twenty minutes of class. Then, once he got settled into his seat, he would ask questions I had just answered.

I could tell the rest of the class was annoyed by it. I was also, not because I minded answering again, but because I felt it took time away from the other students. Though repetition can be good, it can also be frustrating when other things need to be discussed.

On this particular morning, when he asked a question we had just covered, I could hear the sighs of the other students. For the first time, I told him we had just covered that problem.

"I really can't take the time of the other students," I said. "Maybe you could stay after class for a few minutes, and I could go over that problem with you."

"And maybe he could just come on time for once," someone said.

I saw an expression on Trevor's face that I had seen before with some of my students. It told me that something was not right.

"Trevor, could we visit after class?" I asked.

He nodded but said nothing. In fact, he never said anything more for the rest of the class, and he had always been one to get involved in the discussion.

After class was over and all of the other students had filed out, I turned my attention to him.

"Trevor, is there something wrong that makes you late to class?"

Suddenly, tears formed in the corners of his eyes, and he swallowed before speaking. He was a tough-looking young man, and it was apparent he was not used to displaying any soft emotions. When he finally spoke, his voice quivered.

"I try to be on time," he said. "But I have to get my little son to the babysitter first."

He stopped, but I sensed he planned to say more. He seemed to want to get his emotions under control first. Once he continued, the story poured out, and he repeatedly wiped tears from his eyes.

"Eight months ago, my wife and I had a little boy. We had really wanted a baby, and we were so excited. Everything went well, and the first two nights after the baby was born, I held him with my wife leaning against me. Life was so perfect. But on the third night, when I came home, the baby was crying, and my wife had passed away. It was such a shock."

As he continued, remembered reading the story in the newspaper. The young mother had some internal hemorrhaging that the doctors had missed. I hadn't put it together that it was Trevor's story.

"Both my parents and her parents offered to raise the baby until I could get through school," he said, concluding the story. "But he's all I have of her. I need him, and he needs me."

"Trevor," I said, "you be late if you need to. But it is affecting your grade. Is there some way I can help you?"

He was an engineering student and tutored some freshman-level classes. The tutoring was in a classroom close to my office. We worked it out for him to come for help at lunchtime, just before he started his tutoring job. I also asked him if he minded if I shared a little about his situation with the class. He paused briefly but finally nodded.

"I won't share too much," I said.

In the next class, before Trevor arrived, I shared a bit about his situation. Things changed a lot after that. Everyone, myself included, was much more understanding. For a while, he came to my office for help. But then some of the other students started helping him. The one who volunteered the most was a sweet young lady named Melany. By the time the semester ended, I sensed there was more between them than just tutoring.

A few months later, when they came in to let me know about their upcoming marriage, I wasn't surprised.

"Thanks for being so understanding," Trevor said.

I smiled. "Thank you, Trevor, for helping all of us gain a better perspective."

Green Paint

I was dating a girl in high school, but I think her family liked me more than she did. Sheila was quite popular, and I was just one of many boys who asked her out. So, one day, when she called and asked if I would like to spend some time with her the following Sunday, I was excited. I took it as a sign that maybe she liked me more than I thought.

But as she continued with the invite, I realized the reason she was asking me was not necessarily because she wanted the time with me.

"You will be driving your little pickup, won't you?" she asked.

"Yes," I replied

"Good," she said. "I was asked to perform in church, and I need someone to help me get my harp there."

I felt some of the air knocked out of the sail of my ego, but I still thought it was better than nothing.

I heard Sheila's mother in the background. "Ask Daris if he would like to come early. Timmy's been wanting him to read him a story."

Sheila relayed the message, and I accepted. Timmy was Sheila's two-year-old brother. I enjoyed playing with him and reading him stories. More than once, when I was there, Timmy brought me a book, and as I read to him, he fell asleep in my arms.

"Timmy really seems to like you," Sheila's mother said. "He doesn't do that with anyone else outside the family."

I arrived early as agreed, and as soon as they invited me in, Timmy brought me a book. He curled up on my lap, and I started to read. But I hadn't noticed that he had a little bottle of green model car paint. Just as I was finishing the story, Sheila came in and announced it was time to go. Just then, her mom gasped. I looked up from the book and saw that Timmy had poured the paint down one leg of my light-colored suit.

Sheila just stood there in shock. Finally, she said, "Now what am I going to do? I can't get anyone else to take me at this late notice. Maybe I better call and cancel."

"Don't do that," I replied. "We'll just tell everyone this is a new style."

Sheila didn't think it was funny, and all my joking didn't help. She didn't want to be seen in public with me with green on my suit.

Sheila's mom said, "Just hang on a minute."

She left and came back with one of her husband's old suits. It was a fine, older wool suit, but he was much bigger than I was. Sheila paced nervously as her mom did a few pins to help the suit fit better. It didn't look bad, but it was still obviously not my size.

"We better go, or we'll be late," Sheila said.

I loaded the harp in my little pickup, and we were on our way. As we drove along, Sheila told me what she wanted me to do.

"You take the harp in while I visit with other people. Then you find an empty bench by the wall and scoot far in where no one will see you."

"Would you rather I just sat out in the hall so no one knows we are together?" I asked.

Sheila paused, and I could see she was pondering that. Then she shook her head. "No, that's okay. I will probably sit on the stand, anyway, since I'm performing."

We got to the church, and I did as requested. I took the harp in while she visited with people. Then I found a hidden place on a bench by the wall. I sat there through the whole meeting, and when it was over, I waited until most of the people left. Then I loaded the harp.

Sheila's mom wouldn't let me have my pants back. I wore the ones she loaned me, and she purchased a pair at the store, identical to my original ones. She called me and told me she had them and to come over. When I did, she had me try them on. They fit perfectly. As I sat down to visit, Timmy came and climbed on my lap.

But this time, and every time from then on, Sheila's mom checked to make sure Timmy didn't have any paint in his hands.

Thoughts About a Father

I had a good friend and colleague that passed away sometime back. I wasn't much older than his oldest children, so he often treated me and worried about me as if I was his son. As I considered Fathers' Day this year, I thought about him. I thought I'd share some memories I had of him, along with some of his sayings and some things his family shared at his funeral.

Since David and I were both teachers, and I was new in the profession, he knew my pay wasn't always sufficient. He often asked me if I was making ends meet. He sometimes told me where I could get good deals on things he knew I needed. He was a master at knowing about saving money. His sweet wife said that to David, money was not just something that was in limited supply; it was something that needed to be taken care of in hopes it would have children and proliferate.

David tried to save money any way he could. He found four old lawnmowers at the junkyard. His daughter Abby was responsible for team-mowing the lawn with her father each Saturday. By team-mowing, I'm not inferring they both mowed. By the time Abby stepped outside for her assignment, David would have one machine sputtering. Abby would mow with it until it died, and by then, David would have another one running in a half-firing state. They kept this up until the grass was all cut.

Abby said if they wanted something, her dad would provide work, but the work was hard, and the pay was terrible. That was motivation for her and her siblings to find employment elsewhere. When his children would come home from their first day at a new job, usually dirty and tired, David always had to take a picture. And to his children's dismay, the photos were posted prominently in his office at work.

One fond memory I have of David was taking a minute from

my hectic day now and then and plopping in a chair in his office to visit. His office was always neat as a pin. Every pen, pencil, and eraser were in precisely the right place. Occasionally, he would come to my office to visit. I ran all the internet systems at the university and had multiple big servers in my office. My desk was often strewn with notes and to-do lists. David would shake his head and say, "How do you ever get anything done in this office?"

We both laughed at that because I had about twice the workload of anyone else in the department with both teaching and managing the computers. I would always answer the same, "Well, you know what they say, David. A clean office is the sign of a sick mind. At least we both know my mind is healthy." He always took it well, and we had a good laugh at that, too.

David's children shared some fun things about his insistence on order. David was an old army man, and bedroom inspections were on Saturdays. No one could go anywhere with their friends until they passed the inspection. But Jennifer said she found a way to make it easy. Her room was in the basement near the root cellar. She would haul all the items messing up her room into the root cellar. Once her father had passed her on the inspection, she would retrieve them and put them back in her room.

Of all the sayings David used, there is one that sticks out to me. He liked efficient meetings and good use of time. When things seemed to be going in a wasteful, useless, or redundant direction, David would say something that was a cue to the department chairperson to shut down the meeting so we could get back to the tasks we needed to complete.

"When all is said and done, there is a lot more said than done!"

Thanks for the memories, David.

The Ultimate Price

It was Sunday, December sixth. That meant the next day was the anniversary of the attack on Pearl Harbor. At church, I missed hearing Stan share stories about the war. He always did that on the Sunday closest to December seventh.

But Stan's sweet wife had passed away, and he couldn't live alone. He had moved into an assisted living facility. I felt strongly on this day that he could use a visit, so in the evening, I drove there. My eight-year-old daughter loved to go visiting with me, so she came along.

When we got there, Stan was in his pajamas, sitting on the edge of his bed. When I knocked, he looked up. I could see tears in his eyes, but he smiled when he saw us.

After we exchanged greetings, Stan asked, "Do you know what tomorrow is?"

I nodded. "It's Pearl Harbor Day, Stan."

He smiled. "I thought everyone from the younger generation had forgotten."

He looked at my daughter and patted the bed beside him. As she took a seat, Stan said to her, "Don't ever forget the great men and women who gave their lives for the freedoms we enjoy."

"I don't think she has heard many of the stories of your experiences," I said. "Why don't you share some with her?"

"I well remember Pearl Harbor Day," Stan said. "It was just as if it was yesterday."

He then went on to tell about the shock he felt when he heard the news. "The entire nation was reeling from the fact that Japan would act like they were making a treaty as a ploy to throw us off guard, then bomb us.

"It wasn't long before I was drafted into the army. I was barely old enough to go, but my number came up right away. As I went through boot camp, I thought they were trying to kill me even before I got to fight the enemy.

"We finally finished, and we got a couple weeks of leave to go home. That was when I married my dear, sweet wife. Before they drafted me, we had been planning our wedding. But when I came home, we married and spent that short time together. I can remember how her father tried to talk her out of it since I could be killed. But she loved me enough to go through with it.

"Those two weeks were really short, and soon I was back with my unit heading to the war. But just when we were to move to the front lines, they commanded us to line up. We did, and a general pulled up in a jeep. He got out and looked us over. Then he barked out, 'Any of you who have worked with cattle, sheep, or other livestock, take one step forward.'

"I stepped forward, and it was no surprise to anyone that I was the only one in my unit. The others called me 'Farm Boy' because they were all from big cities.

"The general walked over and stood in front of me. 'Have you ever sewed up a cow?' he asked. 'Yes,' I replied. 'Have you ever had to use a knife to cut into a cow to try to save her life?' he asked. 'Yes,' I replied. He looked at me for a moment and then said, 'You are going to become an army nurse.'

"I was so shocked I couldn't speak for a moment. When I did, I said, 'But, sir, I have never worked on humans. And cows and humans are very different.'

The general scowled. 'Don't you think I know that, Private? In war, we take what we have and make them the best we can. You will report to headquarters at oh seven hundred hours tomorrow.'

"The general then left to do the same at other units. The men started teasing me, saying stuff like, 'If I get hurt and moo loud enough, will you sew me up?' But my good friend and bunkmate, Private David

Hansen, said, 'If I get hurt, I'll look forward to seeing you.'"

At this point, Stan paused. Tears poured down his face when he continued. "And I did see thousands of men come through, and we saved many. But for every one we saved, there were others who paid the ultimate price for the freedoms of our country."

Stan then turned and looked into my daughter's eyes. "That is what I want you to remember."

The Ultimate Price
(Part 2)

Stan told my young daughter and me that he was assigned to be a nurse in the army simply because he had worked on cattle. He continued with his story.

"They assigned me to a hospital train," Stan said. "The war was raging, and there were heavy casualties. They gave me almost no training. No one had time.

"I remember my first surgery assignment. It only took minutes for the doctor, who was a captain, to get annoyed with me. 'You are no nurse!' he yelled at me. 'Who told you that you were?'

"I replied that I really was not a nurse, and it was a general who told me that I was. I told him the general said I was just because I had worked with doctoring cattle.

"The doctor was quiet for a moment and then said, 'I see. When we asked for help, we assumed they would send us trained nurses. I guess you will just have to learn.'

"I did work at learning. I watched and listened to everything the trained nurses and the doctors did and said. Sometimes I felt it was taking me forever to understand what I was supposed to do, and I got yelled at a lot. But one day, the doctor I had worked with on that first surgery told me he felt I was learning faster than any student he had ever worked with in medical school. Then he laughed. 'But then, you are training twenty-four hours a day.'

"Sometimes, I didn't feel I was doing any good. But my ultimate goal was to do no harm. Now and then, a critical decision someone made endangered a patient's life, even though that person was trying to do their best. I spent a lot of time praying that I wouldn't make that kind of mistake."

Stan paused as if contemplating that thought. When he continued, he spoke in a more subdued voice.

"One day, a young man came in with a head wound. He was blind, his eyes were bandaged, and his world was dark. He was frightened. He wanted a doctor he could talk to, and each time the doctor tried to excuse himself, the young man would nearly go crazy. The doctor waved me over, then said to the young man, 'I think you need to talk to Dr. Danser.' I started to say that I wasn't a doctor, and he motioned for me to be quiet. He then said to the soldier, 'Yes, Dr. Danser specializes in cases like yours.'

"I sat down by the soldier's bed, and he started to talk. He told me about his hopes and all he wanted to do. I learned he grew up on a farm just like I did. I even shared a story or two with him, but mostly I just let him talk. Soon he relaxed and went to sleep.

"From then on, they gave me the assignment to be the 'Doctor of Consolation' for the soldiers who needed it. Besides my nursing duties, I would listen to those who needed to share their fears. Sometimes it was hard to listen to men who had lost the ability to fulfill their life's dreams when they went home, if they were even going to live to make it home."

Once more, Stan paused, and this time tears poured down his face as he continued.

"One day, I was working in surgery when the soldier that was carried in was my best friend and bunkmate from my training. We did everything we could in the surgery, but the doctor didn't expect him to live.

"Later, as I sat by his bedside, he was unconscious, so I talked to him. I reminded him of the dreams we shared about our lives. I told him about my wife and reminded him he had a girl waiting for him at home. I just kept talking, hoping it would help him regain consciousness.

"I said, 'Remember, you said that if you were ever wounded, you would be glad to see me and know that I was here for you. Well, I am here for you.' Finally, after a few days of me talking to him, he opened his eyes briefly, smiled at me, then he was gone."

Once more, Stan paused. When he continued, his voice quivered with emotion.

"After I came home, I always made it a point to remind people that it was David, and men like him, who gave up their dreams so we could have ours."

Seeing Through the Glasses Darkly

I have been working a lot in the sun this summer, building a shop. I don't think I have been this brown since I was a teenager changing pipe, hauling hay, and doing other farm work. My sweet mother-in-law has been concerned about me being in the sun so much. She was especially worried about my eyes. Because of that, for my birthday, she sent me some dark glasses and a brief note.

"I'm sure the sun can't be good for your eyes, so I bought these to help you while you're working outside."

Even though my eyes are very light-sensitive, I have never worn sunglasses. Since I started wearing glasses, I have always had color-changing lenses. They always work well at first, but eventually, they quit darkening.

The glasses my mother-in-law sent were nice ones. They go over my regular glasses and fit all the way to my face, cutting the light even on the sides. But I just wasn't sure I could get used to them.

"Why don't you try?" my wife said. "You know how much you have to squint in the sun. I think if you could get used to the sunglasses, they would really help."

She was right, and I decided to try them. But for the first while, it didn't go too well. I often forgot to put them on. When I remembered, and someone sent me a text, I had to take the sunglasses off to read it. I would put them on top of my head and forget they were there. There was reason after reason I would not end up wearing them for much of the day. But I felt better during the times I used them.

I decided I needed to make a concerted effort to use them. I still only remembered to wear them intermittently. However, I gradually became more and more used to them, remembering to put them back on when I took them off. I was finally getting so I wore them most of the time while I was out in the sun.

Then came a day when things didn't go as planned. I was transplanting raspberries to some new property we purchased. I dug quite a few different varieties and put them in buckets of water. But just as I was about to go to plant them, some other issues came up. By the time I got those done, it was getting late in the afternoon.

I knew I had to get all the raspberries planted that day, or they would die. I wouldn't have another chance for a few days, and they wouldn't last that long in the buckets of water. I hurried to the new place, put on my sunglasses, and started to work.

I am breaking the garden out of a hayfield. Even though I worked the soil the best I could with a tiller, there is still a lot of grass and alfalfa I must dig through. Planting the raspberries took a long time. I worked steadily, only pausing now and then for a well-deserved drink of water.

At one point, I was just about to take a much-needed break when I realized it was very dark. The sun had gone behind the clouds, so I couldn't tell where it was in relation to the horizon. However, as dark as it was, I was sure it must be just about ready to go behind the western hills.

I looked over, saw all the buckets of raspberries I still had to plant, and decided against the break. I worked as fast as I could, not even taking time to drink water. My throat became parched, and the sweat rolled off me, but I was sure daylight was quickly slipping away.

Finally, the sweat was pouring down my face and into my eyes so much I couldn't see. I had to pause and take my glasses off so I could wipe the sweat from my face. It was at that instant that I realized it was still relatively light. I looked at my watch, something I hadn't considered doing before that moment. I had two hours more daylight than I thought. I set the sunglasses aside and finished the raspberries with a bit of daylight to spare.

When I got home, my wife asked how it went using the sunglasses.

"Well, there's one thing I'll say for them," I replied. "They sure made me work faster."

Animal Fun

This heatwave we are experiencing showed me that animals like to have fun, just like we do. Some things I saw were almost human-like.

I was on my way home from work one day, and as I approached an overpass, I could feel the added heat coming from the four-lane highway below. Even inside my car, it felt like I was passing through an oven. That was when I saw the hawk.

It looked like a young bird. It was floating with almost no flap of its wings. As it came across one of the double lanes of the highway, there must have been thermals coming from the pavement, creating an updraft. The hawk climbed while holding his wings still. Then he came to the grassy area between the two sets of traffic, and he started floating downward.

Once he floated nearer the second set of highways, he started to climb again, with hardly a flicker of his wing. Once he soared over the second set of lanes, he arced his wings, turning to head back across the freeway again.

I had slowed down to watch this beautiful display of graceful, floating flight, and I realized the traffic behind me was getting annoyed. I sped up but kept my eye on the bird for as long as possible. He was obviously enjoying himself.

When I got home, our two golden retrievers came to greet me. Both were soaking wet. We have a large, fenced yard for them, but they have found many avenues of escape as the heat has increased. They make their way to our pond and go for a swim.

I have created a pool in our backyard that they can lay in, and they often do. But with the additional heat, they apparently want to totally submerse themselves. I can't say that I blame them. When I have found them swimming, the ecstasy on their faces showed how much fun they were having.

Sometime later, I was heading home from a town about twenty minutes away. I had just helped a friend pour cement for his house, and the sweat was dripping from me. I suppose that was why my eyes were drawn to a herd of cows all standing in a pond. They looked like they were in a huddle, discussing global warming and their contribution of methane gas to the cause. Some cows, with water halfway to their backs, stood there as if half asleep.

But the event I saw that made me smile the most was a flock of birds. I had just gone past a house that had a sprinkler going. The children were taking turns running through the water, after which they would all laugh as the person shivered.

I smiled at the fun they were having. I hadn't driven very far when a bird swooped so close to my car that I nearly hit it. I turned to see where it went, and it flew through a sprinkler in a field. The sprinkler was stuck, and instead of turning as it put out a pulse of water, this one stayed in one place, and the water sprayed in a wide fountain.

I slowed and finally stopped to watch the birds. The bird that flew through the water landed with a group of birds on the other side of the sprinkler. The birds all twittered as the bird fluffed its wings, sending droplets across the other birds. Soon another bird took to flight, swooped around, and came through the water, landing and spraying water on the other birds, all to their delight. I watched this for a while and thought about how much it was like the children.

As I finally drove on, I laughed at how animals can have fun on a hot day, just like we can.

Involuntarily Volunteering

The celebration of our pioneer heritage is important in our area. In July there is a musical and a rodeo. But the most significant event is the parade. Every church congregation builds a beautiful float, some taking half a year to complete it. These were always church assignments. But then the directive from the church headquarters came that the celebration would be run as an independent organization because of liability issues.

In our congregation that year, the request was made for volunteers to build the float. But due to the amount of work, no one stepped forward. I was given the assignment to announce in church and our community that we would not have a float due to lack of interest. It caused murmuring in the congregation, but everyone quieted down for the church meetings to continue. But afterward was a different story.

I had the assignment of running a correlation meeting for scheduling summer activities. Usually, there were around ten people that showed up. Most of those attending were the adults and youth who led the youth groups. But on that day, the room was packed with people standing around the walls, with others in the doorways and hall. Obviously, there was an issue of concern.

I tried to act normal as I started the meeting. "So, scout camp is scheduled for . . ."

I was cut off by an older lady named Flora. "We want to talk about the cancellation of the float."

"We had no choice," I said. "It's no longer part of the church, and no one volunteered to direct building it."

From the mumbling, it sounded like some there almost felt I should be tarred and feathered.

"You will not cancel the float," Flora said. "It is part of our heritage. I will volunteer."

Another lady named Vivian raised her hand. "I will also volunteer."

Then Flora pointed at me. "And Daris, you *will* volunteer, too."

The last thing I wanted to do was be on the float committee. But one look at the frowning faces around me told me I had little choice. And so the float building began. Flora and Vivian determined the design, and I hauled lumber and started sawing and nailing. The most significant focus was an eagle fifteen feet high, standing with its feet on an American flag that flowed to the front of the float.

When I finished the eagle, I thought it was perfect. Flora thought otherwise. "That eagle will never do. Rebuild it."

"But, Flora," I said, "I think it looks good. What's wrong with it?"

"Its wings are not pointed enough. It looks like a butterfly."

"But I like butterflies," I replied.

"Rebuild it!" Flora demanded.

I took the wings off the eagle and rebuilt it. When I finished, I thought it was flawless now. But still, Flora thought otherwise.

"It looks like a sparrow with sharp talons," Flora said. "Rebuild it."

I sighed at the thought of doing it again. Just then, a big, beautiful hawk flew into the potato cellar where we were. It was probably searching for a place to cool off from the heat outside. It flew up and landed on the eagle.

"Look, Flora," I said. "The hawk loves my eagle."

"A hawk shouldn't love an eagle," she replied. "It should be afraid the eagle would tear it to pieces. But when it looks like a sparrow, all the hawk wants to do is eat it for lunch."

I rebuilt the eagle.

Flora felt it could still be better, but she said it would do. I continued building. There was the frame for the flag, a turntable for veterans to stand on, and many other things. I thought we would never finish. But finally, the day before the parade, with the last bit of trim added, Flora declared it finished. And with Flora's keen eye for detail and Vivian's knack for color matching, it was beautiful. We even won first place.

And now, though I try to help on the float each year, I work with the musical so I will be too busy to be involuntarily volunteered for the float committee.

Lending a Helping Tractor

I grew up in the last house on the edge of miles of open rangeland. Our nearest neighbor was about a mile away. Since cell phones were still unheard of, it wasn't unusual for people who didn't know that country to get stuck and come walking in to our house.

One winter night, around nine o'clock, just as we were heading to bed, a man came walking in. We had just had the first snowfall earlier that week. It was just enough to encourage someone with a big pickup to take the challenge of dirt-roading through it. This man had gotten stuck about ten miles beyond our house. The man was shivering from the cold, so my father invited him in by the fire. While he warmed himself, my mother got him a cup of hot chocolate and some cookies.

"Would you like me to get my tractor and come pull you out?" my dad asked.

The man shook his head. "I have a friend with a big pickup. If you don't mind, I will just call him."

The man used our phone to call, and about twenty minutes later, a pickup with a loud engine pulled into our yard. The two of them left, and we went to bed.

Around one in the morning, there was another knock at our door. My father threw on a robe and went to answer it. Standing on the doorstep were the two men, shivering from their long walk. Once more, my father invited them to warm themselves by the fire while my mother warmed hot chocolate and pulled out some more cookies.

My father again offered to pull them out with our tractor, but they refused the offer. They said they didn't want to be any bother.

"I have a friend with a big tow truck," the first man said. "If we can use your phone, we will just call him."

It took them a while to rouse their friend, so it was most of an hour before he came. But eventually, a big tow truck pulled into the yard. The two men left our house and climbed into the cab with their friend.

At about five o'clock, while we were eating breakfast, there was another knock on our door. There stood all three men, shivering in the cold. Once more, my father invited them in to warm by the fire. My mother warmed some hot chocolate and added some more pancakes, eggs, and hash browns to the griddle.

Afraid it might sound like an "I told you so," my father said nothing about the tractor. But once the men had eaten and were warm, the first man spoke to my father.

"Is your offer for help with your tractor still available?" he asked.

"Yeah," the second one chimed in. "He's pretty well out of friends with big trucks."

The third man, seemingly miffed about being pulled out of his warm bed in the middle of the night, said, "Heck, he's pretty well out of friends."

My father told us to start working on the chores, and he left with the three men stuffed into the tractor cab with him. Experienced on the rangeland, Dad knew how to avoid getting stuck. In about an hour, he was back, and the three men were on their way to their warm beds.

A few days later, there was a knock at the door. When we looked through the window, there stood the three men.

"I sure hope they're not stuck again," my father sighed.

They weren't. They had brought some gifts. There was a toy tractor, a big container of hot chocolate, lots of cookies, and a multitude of thank-yous. But they weren't the last ones we pulled out.

As long as there are big trucks and inviting mud and snow, people will continue to take the challenge.

The Hand of Providence

Hannah had worked a long shift at the fast-food restaurant and was ready to get off when a big rush came. Her manager needed her to stay to get through it. She tiredly nodded and kept the drive-up headset on.

The long line made people irritable, and they often took it out on her. Sometimes they yelled at her or even swore. And some couldn't find their money, changed their order, or did other annoying things that slowed the line down.

At one point, Hannah heard the roar of a motorcycle come across the headset. She looked at the camera and saw a man dressed in all leather. His jacket had a skull and crossbones split across on the two sides of the open zipper. He had no shirt under his jacket, and his chest sported tattoos that were inappropriate for the general public.

The man had a massive beard, and his hair bushed out down to his shoulders on all sides. He revved his engine again.

Hannah rolled her eyes and asked, "May I take your order?"

The man placed his order. Hannah could see that half of his teeth were missing, and the few that were there were black. Hannah shook her head in disgust. She told him the price, and he pulled up into the food line.

In the line behind him was another vehicle and occupants that made Hannah sigh deeply. It was a minivan, and Hannah could see a couple of children staring through the window, with more on the seat behind them. One child was crying, and another was screaming.

Hanna took a deep breath and asked, "May I take your order?"

The women started to speak, and the crying and screaming children grew louder. The mother turned, and her voice was muffled, but Hannah could still hear her over the headset.

"Everyone be quiet or they won't be able to hear me order the food."

The screaming child calmed down a little, but the crying child continued as before. The mother then turned back to the microphone.

"We would like six of your cheapest hamburgers and seven waters."

Hannah punched in the order, trying not to let her tired emotions get the best of her. "Is there anything else?" she asked.

"That will be all," the woman said.

Hannah told her the price, and the lady pulled her van forward in the line. The line kept moving, and eventually, it was the motorcycle rider's turn. He paid for his order, and Hannah handed the food to him. She was about to shut the window when he spoke to her.

"Excuse me. I would like to pay for the lady and children in the car behind me."

Hannah was shocked. Not because that hadn't happened before, but because she couldn't imagine a man like him doing that. She told him it was six dollars and thirty-six cents. He paused a moment as if thinking, then handed her his credit card. Hannah processed the payment and handed the card back. Still, the man did not drive on.

"I think they need more than that," he said. He reached into his wallet and pulled out some money. "Please give this to them."

He handed Hannah the bills, then drove away. By this time, other workers had seen what was happening and gathered around. Hannah opened up the money and found five hundred-dollar bills. She gasped, as did everyone else.

When the car pulled up, the lady held out six dollars. "Hang on. We're trying to find some change for the rest."

When Hannah told her the man on the motorcycle paid for their food, the lady looked shocked. But when Hannah handed her the money the man left for her, the woman started to cry. Hannah counted six children in the car and realized the mother had ordered nothing for herself.

"Would you like to order some more food?" Hannah asked.

The woman nodded and did. Then she pulled around to a parking spot until they could get it for her. Hannah insisted on taking it out. When she handed it to the woman, the woman cried again.

"My husband was recently killed in a car wreck," she said. "I'm moving my family across the country to be near my parents. But I'm out of money. We even had to sleep in the car last night. I prayed for help, and providence has provided it. But the worst part is, I judged that man and thought how terrible he must be. I'm so wrong."

Hannah smiled. "I think he showed us there is good in everyone."

If you enjoyed this book, please leave a review on Amazon at:

https://www.amazon.com/dp/1629860263

Would you like to see the Life's Outtakes column running in your local paper or magazine? Suggest it to the editor. If an editor runs the Life's Outtakes column due to your suggestion, we will send you a free autographed book by Daris Howard. Find out more here:

http://www.darishoward.com

Read stories, purchase books, or subscribe to our short story list by going to

http://www.publishinginspiration.com

Daris Howard's Amazon page:

http://amzn.com/e/B004H76UGK

For inspiring plays and books, as well as discounts for booksellers, go to

http://www.publishinginspiration.com

About the Author

Daris Howard, an award-winning author and playwright, grew up on an Idaho farm. He was a state champion athlete, competed in college athletics, and lived for a time in New York.

Daris has worked as a cowboy, as a mechanic, in farming, and in the timber industry. He is now a college professor. He has also been a scoutmaster, having up to eighteen boys in his scout troop at a time. In his wide range of experience, he has associated with many colorful characters who form a basis for his writing. Daris has had plays translated into German and French, and his plays have been performed in many countries around the world. For many years, Daris has written the popular column Life's Outtakes, which consists of weekly short stories and is published in various newspapers and magazines in the US and Canada.

www.ingramcontent.com/pod-product-compliance
Lightning Source LLC
Chambersburg PA
CBHW050743230626
47052CB00004BA/1106